THE DISAPPEARANCE OF GREGORY PLUCKROSE

THE DISAPPEARANCE OF GREGORY PLUCKROSE

ELIZABETH GUNDY

OPEN ROAD

INTEGRATED MEDIA

NEW YORK

ISBN 978-1-4976-3814-3

This edition published in 2014 by Open Road Integrated Media, Inc.
345 Hudson Street
New York, NY 10014
www.openroadmedia.com

They sailed away for a year and a day,
  To the land where the bong-tree grows;
And there in a wood a Piggy-wig stood,
  With a ring at the end of his nose,
      His nose,
      His nose,
With a ring at the end of his nose.

Edward Lear

1

LET ME MAKE CLEAR FROM THE OUTSET, I DETEST adventure.

It's tasteless, showy, vulgar, and uncalled for.

This having been said, let us plunge to a time not long ago, and two islands approachable only by boat. The first resembles a crocodile, sunning in the warm Caribbean, slumbering, smiling, waiting with open jaws; the second rises like a serpent from the cold North Atlantic, its silver scales composed of sea-weathered mansions of a more opulent era.

On this privileged island (six miles off the Maine coast, where ocean breezes float in from each terrace, yachts dot the sheltered harbor, and no cottage is younger than the income-tax act or boasts fewer than twenty-eight rooms), an art show was, at the moment, in progress.

"That Indian," insisted Houston oilman Clayton Blunt, planted in front of a superb Remington, "is holdin' his tomahawk wrong. If he really wanted to kill the guy ..."

Or was it the Indian's leap that was faulty? I don't recall the specifics, except to say that my employer described at remarkable length the proper way to attack with an ax, while I kept wishing I had one.

To be fair, I have to say that though Blunt was impossible in public, he wasn't such a terrible chap in his own world, on the back of a bucking rodeo bull.

Fuffie Blunt nodded sagely. Their son and heir, eight-year-old Clyde, was staring, price list in hand, at a heroic early Homer as if it were a Popsicle. Son, like father, was not a bad sort, when kept to video games and ponies, but public appearance tended to bring out the family foibles. "Eighty-five thousand," he yelled, "can I have it?"

Having recently purchased one of the finest old residences in the summer community, my employer would presently purchase some of the finest art in the country; now he strode from painting to painting in his eleven-hundred-dollar boots and ten-gallon hat, a good-natured cowboy who liked to own masterpieces. Fuffie paused at a starkly poetic Hopper, striking her patroness-of-the-arts pose, and inquired loudly, "D'you think it's worth a hundred thousand, Gregory-pie?"

"The question, Fuffie darling," I replied, "is do you love it?" As family art consultant and interior designer, these painful conversations were part of my day's bread and butter, a diet of exquisite torture. There was no denying the Blunts a certain flagrant charm, and they frequently gave me extravagant bonuses, in the hoof-and-mane category . . . "*I* love this one!" declared Clyde, from the top of his tiny lungs, combining his father's boisterous bonhomie with his own eight-year-old greed to stuff every penny candy in sight into his brown paper bag, including one N. C. Wyeth. "Sixty-five thousand," he shouted.

The other art lovers at the show, speaking in whispers, had little chance of examining the prices, since Clyde had lifted the list; however, they could listen as he announced each figure and, indeed, had no choice, thanks to the carrying quality of the Blunt voice.

"Now you take that Salvador Dali of ours," Clayton was saying to Fuffie, "the largest Dali in the world . . ." It sounded like a chunk of real estate or thick steak. And if size didn't strike the right tone, Clayton would criticize a priceless possession in a way that made it seem the masterpiece had been done by one of his cowhands. But, as I say, he was a nice guy, which is why I suppose I stayed on; he could slap you on the back, buy you a saddle blanket, and make you feel like a man of the earth.

Beneath the din of Clayton's discourse, I chatted with the

gallery owner, a friend from old, whose barely lifted left eyebrow spoke volumes: *Really. Those Blunts are beyond human endurance. But terribly renumerative,* n'est-ce pas?

I knew in that instant I'd had it. I'd witnessed these scenes with my employers too many times; I could never witness another. It was too degrading in spite of the money. The awful aura of the Blunts was the awful companion of my days and, occasionally, my nights; this was not what Gregory Pluckrose wanted of life.

My warped mirror reflection, the elegant gallery owner, was saying, "I've been meaning to tell you how much we all adored what you did with Kiki's place in the Hamptons. It's so timeless and yet so Kiki . . ."

"I haven't been to the Hamptons in ages," I said, and then in lower tones as we settled down in a pair of slipper chairs covered with Dorothy Draper cabbage roses, "This has not been a fabulous year."

"In debt again?" asked Roger. His shoes especially had an air of sincerity.

"With nothing to show for it. You know how small my apartment is, and how frugally I live, yet my monthly bills are the price of the average American automobile."

Roger glanced around the sea-scented salon. "You work with nabobs and think you ought to spend the same way. I long for my three rooms in New York and reality."

"I'm afraid I can't return to my three-room reality."

"Are they tearing down the building?"

"The woman next door has been playing the same record over and over for a solid year."

"Evoking a love that has ended. She's bound to get over it."

"But will I? I'm not as young as she. I know every word of the song, every chord, every pause, every last bit of cheap emotion has been wrung out of me. I come home at night with my own broken dreams, shattered to the core from some hopeless passion and wanting only healing oblivion. And on comes the record. After putting on the record, she walks, heavily, into the kitchen and makes herself some tea; I walk into my kitchen and make *myself* some tea. She sits at her kitchen table and sobs; I sit at *my* kitchen table and sob. It's like a duet from *Tristan und Isolde*."

Roger's antennae silently circled the room for the hum of a serious purchase before he turned his attention back to our conversation. Crossing his ankles (and confidence-inspiring shoes), he said, "*My* next-door neighbor is writing a sequel to the New Testament. He takes dictation from the angels in ancient Hebrew and occasionally indulges in patriarchal rages against my bath."

"Roger, do you never find life, in spite of its incomparable attractions . . . somewhat solitary?"

"The last time I felt lonely I bought a Tang dynasty unicorn as big as a phone booth."

"I must see it."

"Perhaps you'll buy it. Impeccable provenance. Stolen by an idealistic fanatic in Peking during the cultural revolution, after which it wended its way to Geneva, and subsequently ..."

"How does one accept the realization that one is never going to have a life's companion?"

"By looking at those who do. For example, my next-door-neighbor-the-patriarch married a delightful woman and said to her, 'I will never make you cry.' Which, of course, she hasn't, because she's too terrified, seeing as she's living with a raving prophet."

"What does he have against your bathing?"

"I run the bath once a day, twice at the most. But it seems the angels object to the sound of water."

"Pluckrose," bellowed Clayton, "I wanna give you a lesson in somethin' us cowboys know about."

I sauntered toward my master's call, feeling my flesh start to mottle as I reached him; he was standing in front of a Postimpressionist landscape with horses. "Morgans don't lift their forelegs like that," he said, and he certainly should know. "What d'you think, Pluckrose?"

Clearly, this was no place for a Pluckrose. I would have to take to the streets, which wasn't an easy decision in the face of my earnings and lifestyle. Frankly, I'd been spoiled. From the corner of my eye I noticed a woman of quite another stamp than my employers gazing at me sympathetically.

How shall I say it?

How does one describe destiny?

She was far from young; she was far from attractive in the flamboyant sense. Her sophistication ran as deep as her wealth, and the roots of both were beyond mortal ken—or beyond the ken of a desperate decorator at the low point of his sensibilities. Compared to the Clayton Blunts, she was harmlessness itself, a little old lady who would never, not if the seas ran dry, mortify a man in a gallery.

Little Clyde had joined his father's diatribe against the horses; Fuffie was critiquing fit to bust her silk and snakeskin sweat suit; well-bred art lovers were silently averting their gazes from the extroverted family; and I felt my mottled skin cooling as salvation descended . . .

I managed to meet the woman, *en passant*, in front of a charming William Merritt Chase.

"Excuse me," she said in a low, rich voice, "but if you designed Kiki Ashburton's house in the Hamptons, you must be Gregory Pluckrose. I'm so delighted to meet you. Perhaps if you've nothing too pressing to do tomorrow evening, you might drop by for a cocktail? My cottage is nothing like dear Kiki's, but you might find certain details amusing. Fielding would be thrilled to pieces. Then you will come? How marvelous."

"Gregory," shrieked Clyde, "you and I can go now and get ice-cream sodas."

I was swept out of the show by my oilies, but "Mrs. Fielding F. Hale" reverberated in my heart like the song of the lark. *Pluckrose*, I said, *your suffering is over.*

Which shows how little I knew of suffering.

* * *

"A man in possession of himself," remarked Roger, as we strolled down the lane past a rotund gentleman at peace in front of his trailer. The trailer was decorated with giant plastic butterflies in flight, and the grounds around were graced by a flea-bitten hound, a crowded clothesline, a couple of tricycles, a pile of firewood, and the man himself gazing out at the day, cigarette gathering ash at his lips, shirt and pants partially buttoned, boots partially laced, face partially shaved, and unequivocal wholeness radiating from him and his *mise en scène.*

I eyed the myriad mysterious mechanical parts cluttering the gentleman's yard; a man in possession of himself, he would take apart anything; he would take apart a computer if he had to; and if anyone came into his yard and made trouble, he'd take them apart too.

I walked down the lane, vaguely hearing Roger's conversation, but plunged into mythical realms. *I* would never stand gazing out at the day in peace, with a three-inch ash on my cigarette, a crowded clothesline, a couple of tricycles, and a hound . . . yet it was the life I yearned for most, for that incomparable quality—*a man in possession of himself*—*that* a designer never finds because he's always struggling for it, conscious of imperfections, restlessly arranging and rearranging the stuff of life to create that unequivocal wholeness belonging to the rotund gentleman in his yard.

It's set at birth, you know. My earliest memory is of an infant Pluckrose attempting interior decoration in the crib. I can feel the sunshine streaming through the windows, as I stand unsteadily in my cage, painting its hard wooden bars with my toes. (It wasn't exactly paint, of course, one could only use what was at hand, which must've been a trifle disgusting, but, alas, one's first attempts at art are always clumsy.)

"Yes," said Roger, "Julia Hale's a peach. But in my experience, every peach has its pit."

We'd long left the man, the trailer, and the lane, and were entering the restaurant on Front Street, a grocery cum gas station cum second-hand bookstore (a couple of shelves of tattered romances) and the island's only eatery.

The first booth was filled with fishermen, the second by an infant birthday celebration; Roger and I claimed the third, which set in the window, protected from the street by plastic lace curtains; we could see out, but no one could see in.

"Try the raspberry pie," advised Roger, and gave our order.

". . . You were saying about Julia Hale?"

Outside on Front Street, a sluggish parade made its way through the heat of midday—locals, cottage owners, and parties from yachts anchored in the bay. Three rather odd figures walked slowly by, passing quite close to our gaze: a lady of stern countenance beneath a bamboo sunshade, a white-flanneled old gentleman with a cane, and a pale convalescent shape between them.

"Who's that with Dick DePardo?" I asked.

"I don't see Dick DePardo. The parasol you're staring at is Helen Newhouse and the cane is Teddy March."

"Well, that's Dick DePardo teetering between them."

"There is a certain resemblance. I suppose he could be Dick DePardo's grandfather."

"Look more closely, Roger, and you will see the result of designing an apartment for Babes Rollencamp." The enfeebled figure was lighting a match for the old gentleman's cigarette; his own cigarette trembled between bluish lips. "I warned him against taking the job, but it was his first important project ..."

"You're right," said Roger, "that is Dick DePardo. What in the world did Babes do to him?"

"Changed her mind eleven times a day, treated him like offal, and refused to pay. He tore down walls for her, she wanted them back in place. She decided to move the bathrooms after the plumbing was in. She tried to make him shift structural beams. With a client like that, all you can do is quit. But Dick was the boy wonder fresh out of school ..."

"He's not fresh anymore," said Roger.

I gazed sadly at the formerly youthful figure walking with unsure gait between the striking woman and elderly gentleman. "He was standing in Babes' dining room. He and a team of house painters had just spent two days getting exactly the right shade of taupey-mauve—not, under any circumstances, to be confused with mauvey-taupe—when Babes burst in with a head of Bibb lettuce. 'This is exactly the color I want,' she said, 'and be sure you capture the dewdrops.' It was the dewdrops, I feel, that did it. He snatched up the head of Bibb, flung it at the wall, then took a cleaver and made lettuce slaw, on Babes' ivory-and-tortoiseshell Boulle commode. It had belonged to Louis XIV. We nursed him for three months, in shifts. During my shift he hallucinated that he was Boulle, trying to construct commodes for the Sun King out of vegetables."

The three shapes were far up the street now, but even from behind one could sense the woman's sternness under her parasol, and the elderly gentleman was gesturing with his cane in a most irascible way. "I fear I'll be nursing poor Dick again. Until he dies from old age at twenty-four."

The raspberry pies arrived. Roger thoughtfully stirred his coffee. "In any event, Julia Hale won't give you a nervous breakdown."

* * *

"My dear," Julia liked to say, "I'm just a little old lady with emphysema," but really, a woman of seventy, with vivacity and charm and a couple of face-lifts, is young indeed—at least on an island of *fin-de-siècle* mansions, or on boats of a certain size. By the time you can afford, and what's more have the time for, the nautical motif twelve months of the year, you've retired your chairmanship of the board. (Fielding had retired only a year before, so in their set Julia and Fielding Hale were practically children.)

Even among the evening's gathering, as exclusive a collection of bluebloods as ever tottered through gin and tonics, Fielding was impressive. With his large ruddy face, white turtleneck sweater, and voice that had made half a century of corporate directors tremble, one felt the twilight of the gods; "stunning" would not be too strong a word.

"My dear," said Julia, urging me to indulge in cookies if

I was one of those who must have sweets with champagne, "I'm simply dying to know what you think of my things."

Slipping a cream silk arm through mine, she led me around the party's fringes, both of us keenly aware that what I thought of her place would determine my immediate fate, at least for the rest of the summer. Little did we suspect that sinister Fate had her eyes on eternity.

The cottage was a jewel of its style, namely stone-and-shingle neopastiche elephantine, built in 1890 by the same deranged gentleman who designed the old yacht club and featuring the same marvelous caprices of Queen Anne-John Calvin Stevens-and-whatever-he-could-think-of in the way of turrets, balustraded balconies, and a bit of a lighthouse affair at the end. Filled with chintz-cushioned wicker and portraits of dogs, it was almost too perfect to touch, but I murmured, as if not wanting to say it but sympathy tore the words from my breast, "If only I'd met you sooner."

You could see her worst fears had been cruelly confirmed; her surgically lifted visage colored as if struck; her large, presbyopic, blue eyes grew dark with determination; I could smell my incipient employment in the intensification of Bal à Versailles pouring out of her pulse points. "I've done nothing," she declared. "It was exactly this way when Fielding's mother passed on."

"Then you can't be blamed, can you?" I said with only the faintest hint of not quite believing her utterly.

The house received me. As I strolled with Julia from parlor to hall, I felt the eyes of the painted dogs upon me, and their noses appeared to point with the breeze. They seemed to sense something ahead for me and their mistress, some lovely romp through a bright field of flowers; how could I know what they sensed was an imminent race for our lives? Portraits can't speak or whimper; they warn us only with their melancholy eyes.

Let me hasten to say I had no intention of destroying this marvel of Gay Nineties madness. After the Blunts' crude-oil approach to decor as investment portfolio, the Hales' portraits of dour hounds and setters and late lamented

Skye terriers fairly shimmered with authenticity. My sole intention was to save the month of August, and if that entailed a few unobtrusive additions to the basic theme of dog idolatry and wicker, additions which would make Julia feel her cottage was quite as it should be (which indeed it already was), where was the harm?

I followed the dead dogs' mistress into the house's deeper recesses—cool, unused chambers of faded curtains and echoing floorboards.

"This was Fielding's when he was a boy," she said, showing me a structure of logs, a little toy compound in which her husband had long ago imprisoned some tiny iron tailors, who still gazed out of their black-barred windows into the beam of sunlight that crossed the darkened room.

These old places by the sea, with thirty rooms of memories and ninety summers' ghosts, how seductive they can be. One hears the shouts of children in white sailor suits, their delicate costumes now moldering in camphor, and senses the coming and going of invisible servants whose numbers decrease as the children grow older, as doors are closed and chambers left empty, until finally only one imperious crone and one elderly Pekinese remain; then no one; and neighbors wonder if ruin will reign or oil money snap up the place for a song; what relief when the seventy-year-young son swoops in, what joy for the cottage's venerable soul when an understanding, sensitive decorator walks through its rooms.

Julia led me down a few steps and along a gallery to the next wing. Collections of tropical baskets lined walls hung with devil masks and sorcery rattles. "We brought them back from cruises. Fielding's mother, poor dear, seemed to like them."

Fielding's mother, poor dear, had allowed her cottage to serve as a grab bag for generations of travel mementos. How many summer homes are filled with these silly collections bought on the spur of the moment and of too little use or merit to keep in one's winter residence?—seashells, beach glass, children's fads, things found on a picnic during the twenties—evocative, unpretentious, personal, and jolly.

But the baskets gave me an odd feeling. I kept seeing a head in one of them. (Naturally, it was just a hairy coconut with eyes of seed when I stared at it straight-on, but from the corner of my gaze it again looked like a head.) Well, I'm not superstitious, I thought.

I should have been.

Julia led me deeper still into the house, which wrapped its century-old arms around me, murmuring how glad it was to be appreciated and wasn't I wonderful to perceive its terribly passé but delightful allure? Everything was solid and real, the Dutch doors to the guestroom in the lighthouse, the leaded casements open to ocean breezes, the blue basin of fresh-cut beach roses, the heavy linen hangings in front of a wardrobe designed to let clothes breathe in spite of sea dampness; in the adjoining bath, all marble and oak, stood a fireplace with a niche containing a Wedgwood cauliflower teapot.

I'll take it, I said to my reflection in the round beveled mirror.

And then my face wasn't there.

"Needs resilvering," sighed Julia. "Dingy, dingy ..."

Of course, I thought, the mirror just needs to be silvered.

And there I was once more in its tarnished depths, a bit shadowy but definitely of the living—fair-haired, fair-eyed, slim, soigné, intense, *un peu* highly strung. "Let me show you the Green Room," she said. "Dear Herbert always preferred it." Herbert turned out to be Hoover.

The cottage rambled along, graceful and zany, offering odd-angled chambers, twisty stairs lined with quaint souvenirs, and landings which looked out at the tops of azaleas. Though feudal in size, the retreat was modest in setting, far back from the road, hidden by trees from prying eyes; the rear of the house was exposed to the bay, but only Fielding's friends sailed there. We stood at an open window above the piazza from which drifted sounds of the party.

"Please forgive me," murmured Julia, "but I suspect your position with the Blunts might not be, how shall I say, quite in the deepest sympathies with the fineness of your nature." This embarrassing prologue was abruptly cut short by the thrilling voice of Fielding, bidding good-bye to early departers and announcing, clearly if wordlessly as a gong, that it was time for all other good citizens to follow.

"Do stay," Julia begged softly.

And stay I did, by her side, faithful as one of those damned painted dogs on her walls, to the last lurid chapter of the tragedy.

2

"RATHER INTERESTING CHINA," SAID DICK
DePardo.

"And rather a lot."

The Shipwreck Museum housed in its one tiny room,
which was scarcely larger than the commemorative bell
out front, the salvage of a single tragedy, an ill-fated
eighteenth-century shipment of English crockery which
scallop draggers had brought up in their iron nets. Dick was
carefully examining a broken soup tureen, while I carefully
examined Dick.

His youthful appearance had fled more swiftly and
irrevocably than seemed possible, his hair had silvered
overnight, and occasionally he glanced over his shoulder
with a sidelong grimace as if to make sure he wasn't being
followed—by a head of looseleaf lettuce, I feared.

"You would've thought," he muttered, "they'd have been
more careful when they brought those bread plates up." I
could sense his sensitive fingers twitching to get under the
glass-covered cases and do some quick restorations. His face
grew more lined with age even as he spoke; he was starting
to look like the last scene in *Lost Horizon*.

The museum was open only two hours a week, so it
might seem a natural coincidence that Dick and I should
have chosen the same two hours to visit; but I had actually
come hoping to run into him.

"Glad you're feeling your old self," I said heartily.

"Now that I've come out of my breakdown"—he stared

peculiarly at a rusty anchor—"I feel like steel that's been tempered."

He felt to me like a steel spring about to go *boing-boing*. "Still, you mustn't push yourself. Don't overwork. Don't get emotionally involved. Stay objective. Let them do what they want. Remember, it's just a job."

"You know it's not just a job."

"I know, it's a calling, like being shot out of a cannon, but you can't let it affect your health."

He frowned with pain at a poorly pieced-together pitcher. "Someone should really ..."

"What exactly do your clients have in mind?"

"Well, it's rather unusual. Helen and Teddy are sister and brother, and rather simple in their way. They're trying to recapture a childhood dream, and I'm going to make it happen for them. The whole feeling is robin's egg blue, very ethereal, very Cocteau ..."

At this point, I knew poor Dick was going to be drawn into some stage set for incestuous fantasy, an impossible will-o'-the-wisp; as if he weren't unstable enough on his own, he would be dragged down by two obvious zanies, to be fragmented everlastingly like shards of cracked crockery dredged from the ocean floor by scallop draggers. And would we ever be able to put him together again?

"By the way, Dick, how're you sleeping . . . ? Eating . . . ? No salads, excellent . . . Do you need money . . . ? Do you need a place to get away for a few days? Anytime you want my apartment, it's yours, I'm not going to be using it for months. It's completely peaceful and quiet, except of course for the woman next door who plays the same record over and over, but she's consistent, you can depend on her, she will never surprise you with variation ..."

"I'm doing fine," muttered Dick, glancing over his shoulder. "Yes, I can see you are. But if you need any help at all, just send up a flare. You'll find me at the Hales'."

* * *

I avoided the eyes of Fielding's mother's painted dogs and took my place in the eccentric household. There was one canvas— relegated to the servants' quarters—that summed up what I unconsciously sought. Executed by some forgotten master of the Royal Academy, it depicted a barnyard in the full impossible flower of pastoral peace, featuring contented pigs, chickens, a goat, and a cow; what looked like Shakespeare's mother's dovecote basking in the background; mud puddles and weeds abounding; and everything drowsing in eternal noon sunshine. The picture was manifestly absurd, its mood of quiet utterly naive, but it radiated that peculiar warmth that lures us in spite of ourselves.

Seated on the charming veranda, deep in original wicker, Fielding, Julia, and I perused maps of the Caribbean:

The Hales' own little dot in the British Virgins was to be the start of our autumn cruise, exploring the Greater and Lesser Antilles, the Windwards, the Leewards, all merely romantic names to me, because sailing at best left me cold; in retrospect it leaves me chilled through the bone. Come winter, we would move to the house in Chestnut Hill and do a bit of redecorating there; but winter never came for us.

Beyond the rolling Maine lawn lay sparkling Penobscot Bay, sprinkled with spruce-clad islands; spinnakers billowed on the horizon. A square-bodied maid in black served tea, with cream for Julia and me and a pitcher of rum for Fielding, augmented by popovers and blueberry tartlets.

"Someone around here's got to be a little fiscally responsible," declared Fielding apropos of nothing.

"You're so right, dear," agreed Julia. "As I was saying, if we repaper the morning room ..."

The veranda was flanked by arbors of latticework dripping with purple clematis. Behind us the French doors stood open; formal flower beds dotted the lawn. And from the bay rose Plaster Rock, a tiny treeless island painted white by thousands of years of bird droppings; here, along with gulls, there nested scores of cormorants, tall black creatures who looked, when standing, wings outspread, disturbingly like

Count Dracula in his cape. The voices of seabirds and the beating of waves against stone made a delightfully primitive background to the ambience of privilege—the tinkle of heirloom tea things, the brittle music of Julia's chatter, and whisper of Edna's black dress as she brought out a vermeil tray of petits fours.

"Art," said Fielding, "is commerce. Never forget it for a moment."

"Fielding's on the board of directors of the Philadelphia Museum," explained Julia.

"I've kept them from buying some awful monstrosities."

"Fielding," said Julia, "has such a natural feeling for light and shadow."

One felt a constant vague rumination; the retired monarch's great battles were behind him, but his keen business intuition was tuned to something elusive ahead, some nameless expectation. Was it canonization he expected, I wondered, this man who employed thousands of Third World laborers at eighty cents a day? He studied the petits fours, bending his giant silver head and famous business genius to the simplest decision; one sensed retirement was a cage in which the old lion paced.

With the air of having resolved a weighty matter, he pushed aside the tea tray, and opened his workbox, from which he extracted an old letter-press, between whose boards were the unbound sections of *Captains Courageous*. Very carefully, he began trimming the yellowed pages, slicing off any fragment of leaf that stuck out from the rest. When he was finished, the volume would be perfectly bound; on first seeing Fielding's library, with its immaculate, tooled leather editions, I'd jumped to the conclusion he subscribed to those clubs where, every month, they send you one of the nine hundred best books ever written, in one of the showiest bindings ever wrought.

"You can take down any book in this house," said Julia, "and you don't have to worry about it falling apart in your hands."

"Books are like fine wine," said Fielding, "they improve with age. Don't you agree, Pluckrose?"

"Gregory's devoted to fine bindings," said Julia.

Fielding looked up from his work and fixed me with his stare. "Have you been to the Beineke Rare Book Library? Now that's a collection of bindings. Hundreds of years old, makes today's stuff look like Woolworth's. People don't have reverence for physical objects. Those bookbinders were artists." He bent back to his work. "You ought to go to that library some time. Yale."

"Is that where you became interested in restoring books?"

"Long before Yale." He frowned with concentration as he trimmed off an infinitesimal offending edge of paper. "I got my bookbinding badge back in Boy Scouts."

Like a revelation, it all came clear. That's what my employer was: an old Boy Scout. I could picture him with his neckerchief, his merit badges, his perfect attendance pin, his youth, his life before him . . .

"Membership in the Scouts," said Fielding, "ought to be compulsory. Teach people the work ethic when they're young. Boy Scouts are an endangered species."

"So true," said Julia. "The maid whom Edna replaced, for example. The welfare people said to her, Tour husband's unemployed, that's to the good, but if you would quit *your* job, then we could really help you.'"

"Your library," I said. "It's a marvelous collection, but it doesn't seem to contain anything written in the past several decades."

"Old age," said Fielding dryly, "exempts one from certain burdens."

As I watched him skillfully trimming the pages of *Captains Courageous,* I saw him not as an industrialist grinding peons to bits, but a silver-headed craftsman, as gentle as any old guild member.

"Well, Pluckrose," he said suddenly, "did you find something to spruce up the den?"

"Yes," I said, "an extremely old . . ."

"Good, good."

Fielding believed in the division of labor, himself at the top and everyone else responsible for their own situation, including the ten thousand Chinese working for him in Taiwan for ten cents an hour pleating lampshades. He ruled quietly, discreetly, his nature rustling softly with stock certificates and currencies, his aging wires still open toward businesses round the globe.

Julia, however, was my raison d'être in the family, to make her feel she too wasn't really retired, but still ruler of her own small domain, changing ever so gently the style of two or three old mansions. Julia's happiness was my mandate.

A spectral butler appeared at my elbow. "Phone call for you, Mr. Pluckrose."

"Thank you, Benson, I'll take it out here."

The voice on the other end of the line was Fuffie Blunt's:

"Gregory-pie, I am fit to be tied. How *could* you abandon your poor little Fuffie? Gregory, is that you, lambie-pie? I'm just settin' on my chaise lounge and seethin'. Wasn't my Clayton generous enough with you? I'm sure he's more generous than that stuffed shirt Fielding Hale and that stuck-up old Julia Hale, they'll never appreciate you, are you listenin', honey?"

"Yes, Fuffie dear." I rolled my eyes heavenward for the benefit of Julia, who cocked a sympathetic eyebrow across the Sevres tea service.

"You hardly gave Houston a chance, sugar. There's fascinatin' people in Texas, real people, not these Northeastern cheapskates. I've got hundreds of the nicest friends who'd eat you right up with a spoon. Why, you'll be writin' your little own ticket ..."

I didn't flatter myself as to the truth of the picture Fuffie painted; but I might've gone had there been no alternative, had I not been fatally charmed by Fielding's mother's dogs and wicker, by the mystique of this thoroughly outlandish cottage, the archaic elegance of darling Julia, and the spacious dignity of a more innocent period. In short, I sensed tranquility with the Hales, a sort of trip back through time to a state of grace. Clearly, such an outrageous ideal deserves to be crushed; and crushed we all were, to white sand and ashes.

* * *

"Mr. Hale was always awful good to us children," said Edna, as she led me into her chamber under the attic. "He really treated us more like his own."

I envisioned my employer lining up the island children and handing out quarters for curtsies. "In what way was he good to you?"

"One day, when I was small, he said to me, 'Edna, if you could have anything in the world, what would it be?' I didn't think twice. Says I, 'A bicycle.' And a week later, there was a red bicycle leaning up in front of the garage, and Mr. Hale says, That's for you, Edna.' He sent special to the mainland for it."

I stood silent, considering this odd aspect of my employer.

"Still and all," said Edna, "I wouldn't want to go off on a cruise meself. It's cozier in a house."

"I couldn't agree more."

Alas, this room of Edna's was far from cozy; it had the bleak gray atmosphere of a cheap boardinghouse.

"There it is," she said. "My graduation picture. Maine School for Domestics." Edna and six other unsmiling young women in starched black dresses and aprons stood in front of an ivy-clad institution in front of the sparkling sea. "Hard tickets, ain't we?"

I glanced from the picture to the rest of the room, and shuddered to think of poor Edna alone here by herself in the evening. I knew from all too bitter personal experience how demoralizing the wrong room could be. "And who's this in the other photo?"

"My boyfriend. We're engaged to be married."

"Tell me all," I begged, moving her spindly four-poster bed till it angled strikingly out from the corner; rather regal.

"He's two months older than me. He makes furniture by hand."

"I must see his work." I carried the little bedside table to the window and placed a chair beside it, so that Edna, in the evening, could sit at her work or reading and dream a la Jane Eyre. "What sort of furniture does he make?"

"Everything. Chopping blocks, birdhouses, rockers."

"An eclectic selection." I rolled the bureau to the bare stretch of wall between closet and sink, which gave some semblance of a dressing corner. "Does he sell from his home or in shops?"

"He sells in a store. I could take you."

"Marvelous." I shook out the rug, and placed it in front of the sink to warm her bare feet when she washed on chilly mornings. "When shall we go?"

"The problem is, my day off is Thursday and visiting day is Sunday. So I don't know when exactly we can."

"Visiting day?"

She brightened. "I know, we'll go on a Thursday. We don't have to visit Tim to go to the store."

"Visiting day?"

"He's in Thomaston State Prison. That's where they're learning him furniture. Look, he made this box for me."

I looked at the little square jewel box, made in the pen, and noted that the hinges were too small for the weight of the lid. Was it an unconscious desire on Tim's part to have easy access to the contents of jewel boxes? Or easy exit from his own box? (Little did I suspect, as I smiled at the flimsy hinges, that I too would soon be imprisoned.)

"My room!" said Edna, gazing around. "What happened to it?"

"Do you like it?"

"Gahgeous!" She strolled round the tiny room, then settled in her Jane Eyre chair at the window. "Maybe when I'm married, I'll hire you to arrange my furniture."

"Let us consider it a date."

"Five years," she said. "Or two for good behavior."

* * *

Fielding's niece Sissie arrived in the rain, the prominent Hale bosom tightly ensconced in the same canary slicker worn by every old salt and preppie young thing on the coast. Her yellow hood, tied under the chin, framed a square puggy face. Her handshake was spiritually superior.

Even Fielding and Julia were taken aback by the shining halo round this apparition, which they'd apparently forgotten in long-distance sympathy and greed.

From the day of her mother's death, Sissie Kingsland had been a continual theme between Fielding and Julia, discussed whenever lassitude set in, over tartlets and tea and maps of the Caribbean.

"Since she isn't married at thirty-seven," declared Fielding, "it's not likely she will be."

"So independent," sighed Julia. "And of quite the wrong political persuasion."

"Let's hope she doesn't leave all her money to the Commies," said Fielding. By Commies, I believe Fielding included the poor, the wretched, the homeless, the tempest-tossed, and others who couldn't possibly appreciate such large sums, or certainly not as deeply as Sissie's beloved cousins, twice and thrice removed, namely Fielding's and Julia's grandchildren, or great-grandchildren, one needn't be too specific.

"We can only offer human warmth," said Julia.

"Someone," concluded Fielding, "has got to do something for that girl."

"And show a little fiscal responsibility," I added.

Fielding glanced at me sharply. "Exactly."

So here she was in person, with opinions enough to inflate an observation balloon, and I, possessing neither the bond of blood nor hope of gain for my nonexistent progeny, was devastated at the prospect of careening for months on the wide-open seas with the beast.

We sat down to supper, and the woman said grace. (As James Strachey once remarked, "I make it a point never to stay in the same room with a Christian." Now I vaguely recalled some talk of Sissie's unfortunate papist tendencies; in her renegade youth, she'd peddled *Catholic Workers.*) Nor was her grace your quickly mumbled GodisgreatGodisgoodwethankGodforourfood, but quite a little sermon on the wing, in which she rendered articulate thanks for all but the sugar tongs, in the name of herself, her dear uncle and aunt, the teeming masses, and, lastly, her "new friend Gregory."

Hearing my name, I lifted my eyes in horror, to encounter the lowered brows of my fellow parishioners, Julia's mildly furrowed with concern for her cooling *potage* and Fielding gravely totaling Sissie's estate, and wondering whether it was worth it.

Presumably it was. "Very moving," he remarked, raising his handsome head and a monogrammed spoon.

The chowder was tepid; I saw Julia thinking she must tell the kitchen, in future, to keep the soup tureened until Miss Kingsland delivered her homily.

". . . No, we won't be spared," said Sissie (comes the revolution), "just because we have an umbrella over our heads."

There are many kinds of charm: Julia's regal warmth, of course; or Fielding's magnetism, which was mainly one of promise (he never actually said anything terribly earth-shattering, but the face, the manner, the voice, all made you think he momentarily would).

Sissie Kingsland, by way of contrast, between sermons and doomsday predictions, told funny stories.

The lobster-and-scallop mousse, so ethereal one wondered if only champagne held it together, was thoroughly ruined by an endless ha-ha about the political situation in Nicaragua, a tale presumably convulsing fellow travelers from Cambridge to Berkeley. The vegetable batons vinaigrette, a treat for the eye as well as palate, were destroyed by a twenty-minute repartee, in dialect, between Jesus and Marx. We needn't dwell on the rest of the meal; suffice to say, the flakiest *tarte fine chaude aux pommes* you ever tasted was turned to Mott's by Sissie's ecumenical anecdotes.

On the other hand, who was I to be critical? Wasn't Sissie's social barbarity—the telling of jokes—merely a manifestation of loneliness?

I recognized the symptoms; we were brother and sister under the skin.

"You know, Sissie, I feel as if I've met you before." "I feel the same way," she replied, "having heard so much about you."

I'd been more successful in my outward disguise—give me marks for show business—but how deep did the difference run?

"Nothing scandalous, I hope?"

"Only mildly," she smiled.

I eyed her again; every gift of wealth, each object given to her by virtue of birth was a brick in the wall that shut her off from the rest of us. No wonder she always had to talk about Humanity.

And what's wrong with talk of Humanity? True, it's boring, but at least it's an attempt. Sissie's left-wing jollity was her way of breaking the walls of her isolation; looked at in that light, the endless ha-ha about Nicaragua was admirable.

"Is your cook coming with us?" she asked, as we drifted into the billiard room, where a fire smoldered half-heartedly against the dampness; the walls were cypress, darkly somber, a suitably masculine background for Theodore Roosevelt and other gay blades of the nineties. Fielding and I lit cigars.

"I'm afraid we must fend for ourselves, sans servants," replied Julia. "But isn't that the whole fun of a cruise?" She gaily lifted a goblet of Chambord. "We'll be living *exactly* like fishermen."

"If only we had their purity," said Sissie, after a breath to digest the bad news. Phrases such as "proletarian purity" rolled as naturally from the girl's lips as "gobble gobble" from the beak of a turkey. In any event, in that finely paneled room, in softly cushioned morris chairs, with raspberry liqueur dashed with cream and the scent of Montecristo No. 1 pure Havanas, one safely knew: We would not be living like fishermen.

Fielding played an excellent game of billiards; the man had so much financial wisdom that billiards was possibly the only investment he hadn't turned to profit. Like others of legendary wealth, he seemed somehow outside Humanity, beyond mortal struggles, protected by a ring of glittering commercial power; his aura—if one may speak of such things—wasn't in the ordinary spectrum of colors, but in the range of precious metals—gold, silver, and platinum; the hands which held the billiard cue appeared more manicured than mere nail and flesh, more dapper and, oddly, larger.

My game, alas, lacked finesse. In my unspeakably wretched youth, there was a pool hall across the street from the dancing academy, and my finest buck-and-wings were compromised by fear of being seen through the window; what would the denizens of the pool hall think if they knew I took dancing lessons? They quite probably couldn't have cared less, but to assert my rugged-ness, I painfully razored skull-and-crossbone tattoos on both arms and filled the cuts with India ink. As we shall see, this self-conscious travesty was to one day prove macabrely significant.

Over his billiard cue Fielding nodded toward the wall and a portrait of a Labrador retriever. "Incurable alcoholic. It started with a saucer to settle his nerves in thunderstorms, then went on to cups. Very sad." The billiard cue shot forward, the balls sharply clicked.

"Some people," said Sissie, "worry more about animals than about Puerto Rican children in the slums of New York."

"Didn't your dear mother," inquired Julia, "once have a Scottie who sang Schaefer beer commercials?"

The subject of drunken dogs (versus Puerto Rican children) was plied desultorily, after which, Fielding read to us:

"A late, dull autumn night was closing in upon the river Saone ..."

Fielding's mellifluous voice swelled around me, as I sank into my cushions, a mug of cocoa in one hand, a couple of chocolate chip cookies in the other, and the tale of *Little Dorrit* to lull me half asleep. Each night the hardened capitalist took up another chapter from this book he'd bound himself, and acted out the immortal Dickens characters while the embers glowed in the fireplace and we became children again, being read to at bedtime.

In that dark billiard room, sunk in our soft morris chairs,

we listened to the sonorous prose and the spirit of Dickens seemed to inhabit Fielding himself; he was of an older era, was himself a figure of enchantment.

The gold-tooled binding glinted in the half-light, and the sinister Rigaud appeared in the flames, and the frightened Cavalletto, and all the marvelous phantoms of Dickens, in the voice of my employer, and the creative depths of the man clearly did not run just to commodities.

As we parted and made for our bedrooms, I felt a ghostly presence accompanying me. It's only Fielding's grandfather, I told myself—a gruff old robber baron to judge from his portrait, the type who was likely to scare you a little at night in the hall as he passed counting his corporations like beads on a rosary.

I entered my chamber, and noticed a tissue-wrapped parcel on my bedside table: Edith Wharton's classic book on interior design, newly rebound, in rich purple morocco. My fingers turned to a favorite passage, in pages sewn so firmly they would outlast Fielding's own frail, human binding.

Touched by the gift, I set it down, then tucked myself under my comforter, and reached to switch on the reading light. On the wall above my lamp hung a painting of two afghan hounds, who now seemed to whimper:

Leave while you still can.

I looked around, fearful of the unknown.

It felt like an old family curse was being worked.

Or perhaps it was Fielding's karmic nemesis, the justice due him after a lifetime of destroying other men's businesses.

The house was in stillness.

I decided to go downstairs for an eclair to settle my stomach.

I slipped from my bed, tiptoed out to the hall, descended the wide, curving stairs lined with ancestral dogs, stepped across the library's Isfahan carpet—and heard a loud creak.

My hand groped along the wall. I switched on the light.

The library was dominated by paintings of ships, nautical instruments salvaged from historical clippers, a fragment of a figurehead, and a large model of a Spanish galleon.

I moved, as if pulled, toward the galleon. Bending my head, I saw that one of the dried old masts of the pirate vessel had cracked.

I touched it; the mast fell to the deck, dragging its black sails on top of it, its delicate wires dangling. I stared at those faded slats of hull and deck, at the tarnished brass cannon; Fielding had built the ship in his youth.

I am not one for omens.

But I do like éclairs, so continued on to the pantry to provide myself with comfort.

I stood at the open pantry window, munching the cold sweet by the light of the stars. There are certain summer evenings that bring back one's youth with a poignancy that's almost unbearable.

Quite close in the cove a loon uttered a long lonely yodel of mourning. Surely everyone feels, in the dark whispering evenings of adolescence, that life will give them a partner, that life will always be summer. It would be quite unbearable if we could see ourselves twenty years later, alone in the shadows, seeking comfort from a chocolate éclair.

A successful designer gathers glittering friends, with whom he enjoys familial intimacy. But, at base, it's a buy-and-sell friendship; again I heard the loon, laughing maniacally. There are certain summer evenings that are quite unbearable.

3

IF YOU STRIPPED AWAY SISSIE KINGSLAND'S political and spiritual pretensions, you'd find the genus known as Athletic Debutante. Her days were spent careening about, making herself red in the face. She could've benefited from tranquilizers injected first thing every morning; I got tired merely watching her activity and avoided the practice as often as possible.

"Let's go canoeing," she commanded, cornering me on my balcony and thrusting a paddle into my hands. (At other times it was a riding crop, golf club, or hunting bow.)

"I don't think so," I replied, vaguely indicating, with a gesture toward papers and magazines gracing the twig table beside me, pressing business demands.

"Why not?" she demanded.

"To be brutally frank, I've no interest in paddling a canoe."

Her square face, usually so puglike, knitted itself into the expression of a Japanese chin-dog, lower jaw jutted upward, eyes startled, unable to understand that we are all made differently.

Gregory Pluckrose is a man who enjoys sitting and reclining; if there has to be any movement, it is toward kitchen or buffet table, plate in hand. Sissie, by way of contrast, suffered from an excess of repressed libido, and I was not about to be its recipient, or augment its unfolding by striking myself in the knee with a paddle.

I dislike people who are forever getting into shape. I am

in terrible shape and haven't exercised since the Truman administration.

"I'll have Edna pack a picnic lunch for us," said Sissie. "Cold chicken and *champignons à la grecques,* artichokes and crusty sourdough bread, Scotch eggs, pâté, Beaujolais ..."

The famous Pluckrose salivation response was coming into play. "But what a price to pay."

"Curry and chutney and sushi," she whispered seductively. "Stuffed grape leaves, stuffed figs, peach madrilènes. Sacher torte and Liebfraumilch ..."

I can't tell you how moved I was that she'd noticed my taste at table. I'd thought she was utterly self-centered, and here the adorable girl had been taking inventory of all my favorite snacks. "If it were just you and I and the Sacher torte," I said, "without the canoe ..."

"Imagine yourself, Gregory, gliding through a beautiful forest. Do you know that woods air has been scientifically proven to have a soothing effect on anxiety?"

Languidly I lifted my hand. I managed, barely, to wiggle a toe. "Do I look as if I'm suffering from anxieties?"

"There were tests done in Japan. Eighty percent of the group felt better the minute they got in the woods."

"Clearly I'm among the twenty percent who feels immediately more anxious."

"You're not one for sports, are you?" she asked in a manner implying that superior families are born in the standing position, croquet mallet in hand.

"I have my recreational diversions," I replied coolly.

"*Diversions?*" she cooed, pointedly accenting the first syllable.

Horrid girl.

But a Pluckrose cannot rest defeated for long. In spite of Sissie's nagging presence, I was able to establish my own routine, leaping out of bed at noon and having a two-hour breakfast on the terrace.

"There you are, dear boy," said Julia, gliding toward me with *Guermantes Way* and a sunshade.

"A very handsome volume."

"Fielding bound this during Watergate."

"Julia dear, I've been meaning to ask you, who is that ancient party who pops in and out of the quaint abode at the edge of the woods and glowers at me?"

She followed my gaze toward the right, down to the little cabin, where the crooked old thing was leaning on his cane, staring suspiciously back up at us.

"Yoo hoo, Junior," she waved.

Junior continued staring glumly.

"Junior Plunkett," she sighed. "He was caretaker here for years and years, until he got so bad with arthritis it took him a week just to mow the lawn. Junior and his frightfully noisy lawnmower were a permanent fixture in the view. Well, what could one do? 'Junior,' I said to him, 'you can keep your cottage for the rest of your life, and your salary. But you must promise me that you won't mow the lawn anymore.'"

The old pensioner offered us one last suspicious glare, then hobbled into his cabin.

"Now Gregory, what have you been up to?"

"I've been studying all morning, figuring out what we must do to the den."

"My dear, I'm so delighted to hear you say that."

"Yes, the first thing we must do is take down a few of the dog pictures, for it's rather like living in the ASPCA, don't you think?" Actually, I couldn't take those staring eyes anymore with their secret and unsettling suggestions of impending doom. "We need something flowery and light, a folding screen of lilacs and wisteria and then a small living arrangement of finches. The den must become a sanctuary for the tired sportswoman." I tried not to speak the name peevishly. "Sissie can go there and reflect."

"Gregory, strictly entre nous, do you feel she's overly athletic for her age? I mean, avoiding her social development?"

"I feel she could do with weighted shoes, yes, and a cup of weak tea with gin in it. For Sissie," I continued, "is one of those girls whose buoyancy is in the way of their emotional finesse. In short, Julia, I think you should drug her."

"Oh dear, she is terribly clubby, isn't she."

"A club is precisely what she needs. But barring that, I suggest we buy her a trampoline, and hope she might bounce off into the sea one day."

It was on the sea, the next day, that Sissie again surprised me. We were sailing across the bay to dine on the mainland, she and I alone on the aft of the deck, with our hosts engaged in nautical nonsense up front. The subject at hand was the two gentlemen who were leasing her house in her absence (why do the rich rent out their homes? I've never understood it, except to suggest that greed increases with wealth, in geometric proportion) and how glad she was to have tenants who would enjoy and appreciate the place.

"My agent told me to store the valuables, but these are people who admire nice things, and I wanted them to feel at home."

"Yes, it's so depressing to rent a house where the best china closet is locked. They barely know you and they assume you're going to smash the china."

"I'm charging them enough rent to cover a little smashed china. And the really good things are insured anyway."

"Do you lease your house out every summer?"

"For the last couple of summers I had to stay there to take care of mother. At the end, her only pleasure was her garden. The two men who are renting love gardens too. They wanted to raise vegetables, so I told them they could dig up the gladiola bed. And why not? Why shouldn't a garden be fruitful?"

"That's awfully kind of you."

"They're interesting fellows. One's a screenwriter, the other's a TV producer. I didn't feel it was any of my business to ask them about their relationship."

"Good for you," I said heartily.

"Of course, I have to condemn homosexuality on theological grounds."

The wind blew through her lank strawberry hair as these remarkable sentiments rang through the air and evening's sunlight burnished her button nose.

I was astounded. "One might equally object to trees on theological grounds, or strawberry blondes, or the weather."

"It's a question of morality."

"Morality is a dangerous thing, and should be contained on uninhabited islands, preferably off the coast of New Zealand."

Our boat, the *Hale Fellow II,* was a miniature replica of the great square-rigged clippers that whitened the seven seas in sailing's golden centuries—a bit of history recreated for the child who dwelled within the corporate heart of Fielding F. Hale. It was Fielding's favorite among his collection, a craft of unusual beauty, but I gazed shoreward toward the Merrymount's rambling vine-gripped buildings, and it occurred to me that I might take a room at this quaint inn for the autumn and so avoid the whole glorious cruise; it was a fleeting, unreasonable, barely acknowledged idea, a lifeline thrown by my guardian angel, which I, knowing nothing of lifelines, ignored.

Coolness was falling though dusk hadn't quite come when we docked. Our captain, Albion Slaggby, a grizzled individual with inscrutable disposition compounded of extreme Down East reserve, impenetrable whiskers, and no teeth whatsoever, fastened our ropes.

I stepped down a trifle unsteadily, taking the warm dry hand Julia reached out to me; Julia's hands were marvelous things, seventy-year-old, bejeweled, gnarled appendages to a youngish woman on whom everything else had been lifted.

Albion shuffled along the dock before us, in his classic faded blue denims, of the bib-and-suspender overall model, roomy enough for two Albions; a peaked cap was affixed to his head in the organic manner of barnacle clinging to rock. He wandered off alone, as we four made our way over the lawn toward the inn's massive veranda, where cocktails were being served.

I spotted Roger at the bar and joined him.

"Have you seen Dick DePardo?" he asked.

"Not for a couple of weeks."

"I ran into him the other day. He asked me what I thought of furniture made of asparagus."

"I feared this was coming."

"How did he get mixed up with that bizarre brother and sister?"

"How do any of us?"

Sipping our drinks, we watched yachts arrive in the slow evening darkness of late August; lights on the harbor started to glow with that shimmery quality peculiar to lamps suspended in liquid. As each party climbed onto the dock, their faces were illuminated in the yellow pier lights, revealing a charm chiseled in ice; they'd gotten to their positions of power not merely via inheritance, but also by way of an inner arctic geography.

"Those Blunts of yours," said Roger, "bought my Remington after all."

"But Clayton thought the tomahawk was wrong."

"I took two thousand off," said Roger, with a certain tightening around the mouth that made one think he'd swallowed an umeboshi salt plum.

Around us, kisses were flying like champagne corks. Everyone knew everyone else. They'd gone to school together sixty years earlier. Their parents, in a more gracious era, had constructed palaces together. Their grandparents had swindled the nation together.

"My dear, how *are* you?" gushed Julia of a creature so old the question was no joke.

"Arthur was nearly boiled to death in the mud at Baden-Baden . . ." The dowager empress Clare, with her fifth husband in tow, carried her chin thrust engagingly forward and powdered her wrinkles a wild cerise; tiny golf clubs bloomed on her cardigan and were appliquéd to her espadrilles, indicating a reckless devotion to sport. ". . . and Penelope's tail got run ovah."

She spoke a mélange of twelve vaguely English accents, slipping dizzily from one to the other.

"She was born in Chicago," said Roger.

"In a generation still unsure of its pedestal."

Lanterns were strung over the veranda but hadn't yet been lit; cigars glowed; jewels flashed on gnarled fingers grasping martinis; a lighthouse twinkled across the bay on the island my companions referred to as home every summer.

"Be careful in the Caribbean," said Roger. "Some of those natives have remarkable powers. Last time I was in Jamaica, a fortune-teller predicted I'd have lower back trouble, and it came true in less than an hour."

"Extraordinary."

"I was dancing the limbo, beneath a very low pole."

A bronzed god of about seventy-five paused to talk to my employer. "Fielding, you secretive rascal."

"I've been hearing some very solid reports."

"A question of comprehensive and flexible strategy," replied the gentleman, who like Fielding appeared to voice his own thoughts without undue deference to any sort of dialogue; his name has been synonymous with wealth for generations.

"*Nouveau riche,*" remarked Sissie after he left. It was just the sort of ridiculous thing she would say, and yet, I suppose, to someone whose family had their well-scrubbed gable home near Maiden Lane at the time of Peter Stuyvesant, any Johnny-come-lately unheard of before the Civil War was sheerest riffraff.

A darkly dazzling young matron, with that just-tumbled-out-of-bed chic, sidled up to Roger. "Will you be a darling and lend me the Mary Cassatt for my party tomorrow?"

"I'll be by to hang it myself in the morning."

She bestowed a royal embrace, and slithered gracefully away. "They say," murmured Roger, "it was her brother who trained her, a pimp from Milan."

"Do you think she'll buy the Cassatt?"

"*And* my Tang unicorn."

Julia was probingly cooing to a rather *nouveau* cottager, "The two things I love to hear about people is how they met and how they found their house."

"She knows as well as anyone," said Roger, "that house,

diamonds, and the works were acquired via a forty-page marriage contract drawn up by the lady's lawyer."

He turned his head to follow the doddering progress of the dowager empress Clare, whose family was long a byword for artistic philanthropy. "They got their start in a modest import-export business. Her grandfather imported slaves and exported opium."

The inn was older even than Clare, with a dining room of extreme draftiness, inadequate lighting, and rickety chairs; we joined the move toward dinner, passing the door of the kitchen, where Michel, the resident genius, stood peering out.

"Air-shipped from Palm Beach each June," said Roger, "to further harden the gilt-clogged arteries of the great."

I threaded my way toward the Hales.

Fresh-faced boys waited at tables in crisp white shirts and black trousers; a girl in Victorian dress played a Victorian piano; the dimly lit chandeliers were kind to the aged sovereigns; the menu was superb; the gilt peeled; it was practically perfect.

And Sissie said grace.

As if the entire restaurant was Our Lord—or Her Lord— she insisted on muttering her banal phrases before we were permitted to dig into the *croustade de fruits de mer.*

Apropos of apoplexy, it was during the *potage aux grenouilles* (justly acclaimed by Michel's admirers and of the most delicate green) that a certain ancient party hobbled up to our table, dribbled a kiss on Julia's cheek, and asked me if I knew Johnny Mercer.

"So sorry, I don't," I replied, though why he should think I would was something I never understood. It was almost a nervous tic; whenever the old millionaire saw me, he inquired whether I knew Johnny Mercer. Conceivably, it had once made its sluggish way through the narrow channels leading to what was left of his brain that I'd once had something to do with theater; but why Johnny Mercer? I could've regaled the poor dodo for hours on any number of performers more of the moment than Mercer, but apparently only Mercer would do. Perhaps the old party had met

Mercer himself? But why the indelible impression on a man who, it was rumored, had made presidents, and surely could have hobnobbed with countless stars? I never found out; so complete was his disappointment on being replied to in the negative that he would have no more to do with me until our next encounter, when hope would spring again in his flinty old breast. "D'you know Johnny Mercer?"

Now he turned his bloodshot eyes on Fielding. "What're your plans for fall?"

"A bit of a cruise."

This elicited talk about trade winds, Beaufort scales, and a particular patch of Caribbean water that "kicks like a donkey." It made me seasick to listen. The archaic language of sails was as foreign to me as the language of finance.

Nor was I the only stranger on the Olympian slopes; at a table next to the window, ensconced between pater, mater, and an elderly daughter recovering from a costly divorce, sat pater's airplane pilot, a rough-cut daredevil of a flyer; what was this young proletarian doing dining *en famille?*

One might as easily ask the same of me.

You can say we formed a counterpoint to the staggering sapphires and jowls, but why was a counterpoint needed? Which brings us back to that rather absurd painting hanging in the servants' quarters of our cottage—of domestic animals grazing in a barnyard, basking in impossible loveliness, peace, and noon sunshine:

The beau monde were the pigs, chickens, goats, and cows drowsing in their anachronistic innocence and pastoral perfection, unconsciously forming a scene so sublimely artistic, it fairly cried out for a witness.

Enter Gregory Pluckrose, witness.

And victim.

* * *

"Gregory," said Sissie, "aren't you worried about your physical decay?"

"I try not to dwell on such things." To be more exact, I was dwelling on the view from my balcony, the ragged isles of

Maine, and mentally rearranging several for better balance; the foreground was rather taken up by old Junior Plunkett, the pensioned caretaker, maliciously skulking about the rose bushes. "What makes you think I'm decaying?" I asked recklessly.

"Your deathly white pallor. And you have no muscle tone whatever."

The woman went straight for the jugular, with no politesse. "Sissie dear, do we know each other well enough for such an intimate exchange?"

"Don't we? You're my only friend in this place."

What could one say?

"How about a game of tennis?" she asked.

"Pass me the racquet," I answered and rose to my feet; I entered the cool shade of my room, locked the door to my balcony as well as the one to the hallway, and drew myself a deep bath in the old whale of a tub.

Sinking into its luxurious depths, I reflected upon Sissie's bizarre statement about our friendship. Could it be that her endeavor to make me an athlete really reflected affectionate concern for my cardiovascular health? From outside came the sound of a tennis ball being whacked around; it gave me pleasure to hear it and meditate on my not being connected in any way with its trajectory.

Looking down at me from the antique pine walls with their transparent wash of Victorian dark green were a friendly pair of foxhounds. The light came gently through diamond-paned windows. I opened the *Times* and sank deeper into my oversized tub, controlling the hot water faucet with my big toe.

There I would remain until my flesh grew white and shriveled as a snail. There I would be hours later when Sissie finished whacking her balls around. Only when I heard her go to her own room and bath would I arise from mine, more pallid than ever she'd seen me.

Muscle tone indeed.

4

"I<small>F WE'RE LUCKY</small>," <small>SAID</small> E<small>DNA</small>, "T<small>IM'LL BE</small> working the store. Odd times he does." And with a queenly gesture, she led us into the prison emporium, myself and Dick DePardo, who desperately needed an outing, though our choice of destination may not have been the most therapeutic.

The furniture was bastard Colonial, overburdened with varnish; the atmosphere was, inevitably, one of confinement, which didn't bother Dick. "Remember the charming room you got me in that rest home? The three happiest weeks of my life ..."

Puttering around with a dustrag among the joke souvenirs was a suave old convict of beaten but defiant air and pomaded silver hair. He looked at us, lifted a cunning eyebrow, and headed straight for Dick with the instincts of a spaniel grounding a pigeon. (I assumed the old con would get no commission, and was merely keeping his skills from rusting.) In short order, he'd interested DePardo in a saltshaker made from one solid block of wood, sans holes for pouring, sans cavity for filling, and an equally solid nutmeg grinder sans bowl.

"But this is superb," exclaimed Dick, holding up the Kafkaesque nutmeg mill as if it were a chalice attributed to Benvenuto Cellini. "Form follows function and then denies it!"

The silver-haired gentleman drew back suspiciously at the compliment; was *he* being taken? But no, he quickly perceived DePardo was innocent. "It's a good joke, ain't it?" said the con chummily. "See, someone tries to salt his potaters ..."

"Joke?" asked Dick, for whom the grotesque object was revelation.

"What I meant was, well let's see, it's smooth, see that grain of the wood . . ." And so the two men found middle ground, on the fine points.

"It augurs ill," I murmured to Edna. "Those are the very items, *je peur*, to set upon asparagus furniture."

"You'd be surprised how popular them little grinding mills are . . ." Suddenly her expression softened, her voice grew rough. "Well, old sock, how're you holding up?"

I turned to see a burly young man with the ubiquitous dustrag. "They been feeding us too much rice," replied Edna's fiance, "my eyes are startin' to go sideways." He looked from Edna to me. "Like a Chinaman."

No introduction seemed to be necessary, nor any reply. "Interesting shop you have." I gestured toward the ponderous tables, tipsy birdhouses, and rakish rockers. All the objects, I was beginning to notice, seemed slightly deformed. It wasn't that the proportions were any worse than mass-produced junk, and the wood was definitely superior, but something was drastically off.

"Has your mum been to see you?" asked Edna.

"She brought me some cod cheeks."

"Lovely," said Edna, while I imagined a pair of cod cheeks, with the famous smuggled file sticking out either end like whiskers.

Tim's own whiskers, or rather his mustache, was large and droopy, but there was nothing droopy in his manner; he was obviously bearing up in spite of the rice. One couldn't help putting oneself in his position, and wondering . . . but there was really nothing to wonder about; in no way could I possibly hold up in this tragic place.

"Is the warden treating you right?" asked Edna.

"Like his own son."

"Things are pretty good then?"

"Can't complain."

"And how's the gang?"

"Harry hung himself last week. Bob got stabbed in the arse with a screwdriver. And Steve got his leg broke in the bars."

"Sounds like pretty poor chewin's."

"Accidents will happen."

I glanced quickly around to see if anyone was coming toward me with a screwdriver, then discreetly edged away from the happy couple.

What was it about the furniture?

I studied a massive maple coffee table. Were my eyes deceiving me, or was one leg considerably thicker than the others?

I examined the Windsorish chair beside it, and discovered that not all the spindles were round; two on the left were squared.

Slowly I moved through the prison store, seeing secret mutants everywhere, and the ominous atmosphere of the place took on the freakish twist of dreaming.

Do you suffer from prison dreams? With me, it isn't merely dreams; as long as I can remember, I've always known I'd end up in jail.

I felt the eyes of a guard boring into the back of my neck. It really is a wonder, I thought, pulling open the vegetable-catch-all drawer beneath a chopping block, that I'm not in prison already—for vague unknown reasons. I deserved to be; there were numerous people who'd like me to be. I'd felt it from earliest childhood, my earliest memory, painting the bars of my prison crib.

The cheerful voices of Edna and Tim were apart from, yet part of my unease. Dick DePardo was scratching himself with a poplar back scratcher as if he had fleas. And I felt like a piece of prison furniture—freakish, malformed, a mad vision from the day of my birth, as if one of my legs, instead of being round, was square. My mind was a loosely hinged birdhouse out of which anything might fly.

Tim was a convict, Dick was insane, and they were getting along fine in this jumble shop of dreams. While I, the celebrated, world famous (in my métier), award-winning Gregory Pluckrose, was terrified.

Of what? Of rectangular rolling pins, which echoed some forlorn design in my own deepest nature? This store, this prison nightmare, was not just a casual gift shop I'd strolled into, but the lost continent of my own flawed and misshapen soul.

This is ridiculous, I said to myself. Why should a showroom of faulty furniture have such personal power? The answer came to me instantly: The conditions of my own manufacturing, long ago, were faulty.

Dick DePardo was peering into cabinets, compulsively opening everything with hinges, Edna was chattering. Tim was more-or-less dusting. And I was telling myself I was free. *Pluckrose,* I said, *you're free. It's Tim who's in jail. And he *has* a relationship.*

Now Dick was taking his shoes off and on with an enormous clothespin-like bootjack. I saw his lips silently moving: "Look, no hands."

You walk into a place, expecting to find the expected items, just as you expect to find the expected about people. You expect them to be shaped and function properly as saltshakers, and you expect yourself to do the same, and you grow up realizing you are the single saltshaker in which someone forgot to bore the all-essential pouring holes.

At last, we made our good-byes; Dick took his peculiar purchases to the cashier, and wrote out a traveler's check.

"Driver's license," demanded the heavily armed guard.

"I don't have one," said Dick. "I don't drive."

"What kind of ID *do* you have?"

Dick fumbled with his charge cards, which the guard examined suspiciously, recording details and stopping just short of fingerprints. By the time we escaped from the store to the yard, Dick's lips were trembling and I was hallucinating my own face peering out between the bars of an upstairs window.

"'Twas a treat for Tim," said Edna as we piled into her patchwork Buick, which was actually Tim's.

"Maybe I should get a driver's license," said Dick.

"First, you'll have to learn to drive."

"It's easy," said Edna. "I'll teach you." She was barreling along the highway quite knowledgeably.

"Suppose I lose control," asked Dick, "and the car runs amok, and I kill innocent pedestrians?"

"Vehicular homicide," said Edna. "Depends who you get for a judge."

"I wouldn't bother," said I. "You may never be asked for your license again."

Dick had opened his package, and was compulsively cranking the handle of the frustration mill.

"Tim makes all kinds of stuff like that. He's something of an ingenious."

"What lovely countryside," I murmured to turn the subject from cranking.

"Vegetation," said Dick and shook the holeless saltshaker vigorously. "The organic flow of Art Nouveau."

"Ain't it?" said Edna agreeably.

Dick sat between us, wielding his wooden purchases. I could tell he was brooding about his incestuous clients. "Teddy and Helen" —*grind—shake*—"don't understand these things."

"We're not supposed to discuss work today."

"Never mind," said Edna. "I'm sure Teddy and Helen are better than the sardine factory."

"I wonder," said Dick thoughtfully.

"It's awful hard on the hands."

"Just remember," I said, "if things get unbearable, you can always borrow my apartment. And," I added jokingly, "if anything happens to me on the high seas, you can have it permanently."

* * *

Between other unsuitable flirtations, Sissie had flirted with taking the veil; even now, the romance wasn't dead. Shortly before our Caribbean trip Julia and I accompanied her down the coast of Maine to a Franciscan monastery hidden in vine-covered majesty between the sheltered village of L-port and the ancient sands of wind-buffeted L-Beach.

Never had I seen Sissie quite so excited. All the way down she'd bubbled with a touching intensity; she wasn't looking forward to merely a nice day, but to a nice eternity.

Both Julia and I treated her particularly gently, as one might treat a child looking forward to Christmas. Expectations are so easily crushed, and human hope is so frail.

With popish proprietariness she strode to the stone sanctuary, rang an alarmingly vibrant bell, and serenely waited for whatever-kind-of-sacraments-were-happening to come to a standstill in her honor.

Julia and I, hovering fifty feet behind at the edge of the raked gravel drive, locked anxious eyes. "Must we?"

"Perhaps we might worship outside," I suggested.

We approached the holy one, who'd given the bell a second imperious peal, and informed her we were going off to admire the grounds.

Her exalted, preoccupied gaze skimmed us lightly, dismissed us, and we hastened away on a path that melted into the woods.

"I believe I hear chanting," said Julia.

"So comforting, chanting."

"We're *not* going toward it?"

I assured her we weren't. A faint silver mist penetrated the spruce; September is mild on the coast, but often the sun is veiled in gray shimmer; when I summered in Provincetown, the artists there used to claim it was solely the luminous grays that drew them back again and again to that carnival; but here was the same strange lighting in Maine.

"I feel a spiritual hand on my brow," remarked Julia.

"Spiderwebs."

"I prefer the term *gossamer.*"

Here and there in the woods sat a bench where an aged monk might rest his obsessions. I gestured chivalrously, but Julia plodded on through the forest; rust needles cushioned our espadrilles.

"There's nothing to stop her now," said Julia. "Perhaps the veil's really the answer."

"She'd probably have to give up her politics."

"I shouldn't think so. With such a large dowry."

The woods opened onto a scraggly marsh, where the trail grew unkempt, as if the splendid monastic tapestry were unraveling at the edges. Gulls now broke the silence, their harsh cries troubling the fog, and the cool ecclesiastic scent of peat moss was washed by brine.

A small star-shaped white flower grew wild along the rim of the marsh.

"Do you know the myth of the edelweiss?" she asked.

"This isn't edelweiss."

"The edelweiss grows from the seed of men who are hung. They ejaculate at the instant of death."

"Small consolation," I replied, but the absurd legend remained in my mind; like spiderwebs crossing one's face, it seemed disturbingly alive. I was never one to avoid talk of death, but the image of those delicate Alpine flowers sprouting silently on mountains where murderers had swung found a home in my dark dreams, and lodged. How could I know why at the time?

The marsh became a thin strip of land, meandering toward a tiny island, on which stood a wooden gazebo. The hazy pewter bay, the open pagoda—we might've been in Japan, at a Buddhist monastery, except it was utterly derelict. No one had tended the place in some time, and either tourists or the tide had deposited faded cigarette wrappings, crumpled potato chip bags, and other souvenirs of contempt on the dying grass.

We entered the gazebo and gazed out at the immortal sea and the nearby arm of L-Beach, where I once slept in a venerable inn and lost my white crepe de chine pajamas in the sheets; when I returned, the inn had been mysteriously converted into condominiums, as if donning a quick (though admittedly costly) disguise to keep my pajamas.

"Were you alone?" asked Julia.

"Does one lose one's pajamas alone?"

She sat leaning against one of the gray weathered beams, her ringed, weathered hands clasped round her knees; her face, so recently lifted, was unruffled as the smooth bay behind her. Julia's skin seemed always to be polished, like an antique with a priceless patina; of Fielding's many expensive possessions, his wife appeared the most valuable.

The term "society beauty" is used freely to refer to any wealthy female less homely than her horse, but from old photos I'd seen, Julia had been genuinely pretty; even now, her profile was touchingly lovely, a work of art well restored. She was slightly dizzy and wholly delightful, with the natural distance of the patrician. One needed only to know, in her company, when to become invisible, or when to say the modest clever thing, a role for which I was innately suited. (From where did I inherit this aplomb? Had I been wealthy in a previous life? A pity I wasn't in this life.)

"He's just like a son to me," I once overheard Julia telling a friend (about me), and then she added, "almost."

The tone of that "almost," rendered in Julia's deep alto, spoke volumes.

One mustn't forget her eyes; in youth a fine royal blue, over the decades these twin cornflowers had faded to the mildest, most sympathetic hue, serving as a consummate foil for a lifetime of deluxe self-indulgence. At the moment, however, as they turned on me, the blue was pellucid: *I know I'm a wicked old woman . . . but would you change me?*

As we gazed into each other's eyes, bells began to peal.

"In need of tuning, aren't they?"

"Perhaps Sissie will buy them new ones."

After the ringing had gone on at some length, we began to take it personally, and drifted to our feet.

"Do they make marmalade?"

"I believe it's the Trappists who make marmalade."

"It's an awfully good location for beach plum jelly. Small batches."

We wended our way across a tortoiseshell lawn, Julia flitting ahead and I straggling behind to admire some statuary, an exceedingly bizarre marble grouping of a wan holy ascetic and several dimpled cherubs beneath the legal age of consent. Lost in reverent contemplation, I heard: "You're needed at the infirmary."

My head swung round; a monk stared down.

"I'm sorry," the young man stammered. "I took you for someone else. I thought you were a brother."

Needless to say, I was hardly clad in monkish attire; I made no attempt to conceal my surprise.

"It was your posture," he stammered. "I mean, your attitude. The aura . . ."

Had the booby actually thought I was undergoing, God forbid, a religious experience?

Little did I realize, in that instant of brief amusement, the booby was a seer.

But let me not jump ahead; it's still September, L-Beach; Julia, Sissie, and I regroup outside the vine-choked vestry; Sissie is so puffed with humility, she hardly fits into the Bentley.

Having paid respects to Rome, we are now borne in ungodly comfort to the village of L-port, to worship the joint idols of Mammon and Chotchka.

L-port is emphatically not boardwalk; its gift shops are quaintly restored nautical buildings of pristine shingle clustered on both sides of the L-River. Nor are its tourists the hot-dog-and-beer set you meet at Old Orchard Beach, but on this particular silver afternoon appeared to be mainly middle-aged ladies of the unguided variety, trudging the reconstructed courtyards and alleys in vivacious duets and trios.

"I always feel," remarked Julia critically, "a fishing village ought to wind steeply."

"But the Riviera is so meretricious," said Sissie.

Though regrettably flat, L-port was literary; the canvas shop was named Canvasport; the brass shop, Brassport; the kitchen shop, Kitchenport; the cardshop, Cardport; like Gertrude Stein, they were not prejudiced against repetition.

Filtering into the opulent hush of the Antiqueport, one of

those spick-and-span establishments where even the oldest globe of the pre-Newtonian world looks like a Sturbridge Workshop reproduction, my charges and I separated to peruse French paperweights and British racing trophies, in eternal hope of finding *exactly what we needed.*

You knew the sconces were polished with Wenol daily and prices reviewed with the stock market quotes; the Early American stenciled, washable papered walls flashed with hunting scenes behind glass, in sets, as well as primitive portraits of painfully constipated colonials.

"Come here," whispered Julia excitedly, steering me toward a bronze nude with wings and other weird things sprouting from its androgynous being. "Gregory, what is it?"

"An unfortunate imitation of a late fourth-century B.C. Etruscan patera handle."

"Not really! But wouldn't it look divine on the little bamboo *étagère* beside the umbrellas?"

I replied it would look hideous beside the umbrellas. Sissie swam by us, bust foremost, snorkeling among the expensive antiquities; she rose to the surface bearing an ebony crucifix embellished with garnet carbuncle blood clots, mother-of-pearl inlaid tendons, and the emerald onset of ague, a sight so frightfully overwrought, one could do no more than avert one's gaze.

"No," I said, and again, "no," as they served me up dubious Crown Derby, even more dubious Imari, and a First Empire *bonnet à poil*—"So masculine," declared Sissie. In desperation I threatened to cut up their American Express cards. "Come this way, Julia, Sissie, please, over here . . ."

(Watch the youthful fool, on a lark, enjoying the lighter side of life. Little does he know what tropic shadows lie ahead. A terrible profile is cast on the fog, but he doesn't see it. Far away, in the steaming jungle, a beast sits patiently, tail curled, waiting.)

I happened to know of a gift shop where it was all but impossible to go wrong, and toward there we turned our rope-soled steps.

A tinkling bell bid us enter the store, along with the

fragrance of scented candles, a perfume so prevalent in trinket emporiums it was almost the smell of mother's bread to me. Amidst glinting chrome-and-glass cases stood a matronly lady quivering in epiphany, having come upon *exactly what she needed,* namely four prancing horses jointly balancing a crystal ball on their pewter snouts to the tune of a thousand dollars.

The good woman was all but neighing; her two fellow seekers, armed with ecru totes from the Canvasport, whinnied their approval; the owner of the tasteful boutique babbled hysterically; it was much like a bride with her maids, all deliriously sharing (the next day, of course) the fervently prayed-for first orgasm.

Celebration swift turned to orgy, with the elderly bride piling purchase on purchase, abated by the shrieks of her friends (and, I'm ashamed to say, Julia), adding silver elephant to crystal horse ball, then a soapstone family of seals. "Ah could jes' cry," she cried, "when ah think how they club them cute li'l things."

"I haven't worn my sealskin coat," agreed Julia, "in thirteen years."

"Ed's gonna kill me when ah get home. He'll say, 'Honey, why do you buy silver fo' yo'self, you know I'd buy it fo' you.' Ain't that unicorn cunnin'!"

The wall-to-wall carpet was moist with emotion, the glass cases denuded, the shop owner delirious, even Sissie seemed moved.

"But Ed hardly ever goes shoppin' with me, which you know fo' a fact, Puddin-Jo . . ." She turned to her friend for reassurance, then a question clouded her brow. "You don't think six seals are too many, do you, Puddin-Jo?"

Watching the bride of the hour recklessly squeezing her last drop of pleasure, one couldn't help but think harshly of Ed, at home among the magnolias, with his hand on his young secretary's leg.

I wanted to take all the ladies under my wing; imagining the dear woman's living room, piled high with jujubes of the trail, was enough to make one giddy. So few collectors are capable of restraint. I've had clients with three or four homes plus warehouses crammed with Queen Anne and *objets de vertu*. I realized that only Julia's awe of Fielding's mother's ghost had kept her from mining the cottage in Maine, and I thanked the muses it was I she chose and not some other, unbridled decorator to make the very few changes.

Surfeited, we took to the street, whose gray coastal light greeted us unkindly, as is so often the case after debauch. There was something in the air, a presence in the brooding fog. The terrible shadow of our future was long, and followed the happy little shopping party.

Unable to bear the unknown specter, I dove across the mews and in through the next tinkling doorway, herding my two damsels before me. We were determined not to be always bridesmaids; we'd buy something, or bust.

The curiously comforting ambience of crowded disorder, crumbling parchment, and moldering volumes engulfed us; the den we'd entered was precariously stacked with estatesful of unwanted books as well as obsolete library accoutrements from mismatched quills to broken whale-oil lamps; how this Dickensian hovel had settled, dust, rust, and all, in antiseptic L-port was nothing short of a miracle.

Here we uncovered the diaries of a seventeeth-century Dominican friar who'd spent six scintillating volumes gallivanting round the Caribbean. Little did I dream that one day the blessed Pere Labat would accompany me to hell and fill what sleep I could steal with nightmares.

We also bought a sea captain's lap desk, lined in purple velvet and fitted with pencil compartment and inkwell. I know this tiny mahogany desk as well as I know my hands. It is on it I am writing these bitter memoirs tonight, as I sit alone in my cell.

Last, we purchased an eighteenth-century letter opener, a graceful silver thing with bamboo-turned handle; a mere stocking stuffer; a whimsy; in that moment, surely, Lucifer grinned; it was this hated trinket which ultimately placed me beyond the pale of my fellow human beings.

Delighted with our fiendish finds, we merrily took to the street.

Across the avenue strolled the three ladies we'd encountered in the boutique buying everything in sight, and the woman who'd done the spending seemed unhappy indeed; in fact, she appeared confused now that her fleeting pleasure was over, the orgy finished, and crystal balls, unicorns, and other marvels winging their way air-freight to her home in Atlanta to further clutter a decor which was already an *embarras de richesses*. Poor unguided woman, I thought. Whereas Julia, protected by me, had only purchased three relatively inexpensive, quite exquisite things, which we really needed.

I nodded gravely toward the unguided woman, murmuring smugly in Julia's ear, "But for the grace of God, there go you."

Was there ever, in this life, such a fool?

Beware, Gregory, says the presence in the fog.

(But, of course, Gregory doesn't listen.

He's too busy having fun.

In the steaming jungle, the beast's tail twitches.)

5

"GREGORY, YOUR DIET OF FATTY FOODS IS REALLY too disgusting."

"Thank you, Sissie, I'm encouraged by that."

"I wonder what your cholesterol level is."

"I wonder if the flamingos are flying to their nests," I retorted, an admittedly weak rejoinder, but she'd just ruined my snack and was clearly bent on ruining my short stay in the Virgins. Sissie, Julia, Fielding, and I had flown down to avoid the cold autumn Atlantic and now awaited the arrival of the *Hale Fellow II* and our dreaded cruise.

The ceiling fan turned slowly, stirring the sweet sultry air where the veranda hung above a grove of fruiting palms; showy double red-and-white bougainvillea, hibiscus, and oleander proliferated; how vulgar nature can be when she chooses.

"Gregory, you're the perfect example of a spoiled male."

"And you are the perfect example of a spoiled egg."

She stared down at me, hockey stick in her fist, wondering what I meant; I meant nothing; I believe the image of the egg came from her mentioning my cholesterol level, which was probably terminal. I gazed glumly at my artery-clogging Napoleon and steaming *café crème*.

"Why don't you try to discipline yourself?" she demanded.

"Have you any ideas?" I inquired with lifted eyebrow. "Is discipline one of your specialties?" I could picture her in a nun's robe, hockey stick replaced by a whip, stalking some twisted dream of love. But kindness forbade me continue.

"There are areas of life," she said, "that *you* have closed off."

"The only area I would close off is the one between your upper and lower lip."

"How dare you," she snapped, reddening to her strawberry roots.

"I might equally ask why you are so nasty to me?"

There was a moment's silence, and then she said in a strange small voice, "Because I'm a horrible person."

I was stunned by this merciless voice of truth within her that spoke. I hadn't suspected her of the tiniest self-knowledge. I wanted to put my arms around her and soften the blow, but before I could, she'd collected herself:

"You've never done one thing that's athletic."

"But I have."

She leaned forward on her hockey stick, gazing at me with greedy interest.

"It's not something I like to talk about," I said.

"Come on, Gregory."

"Do you promise not to tell anyone?"

"I promise." I believe she would've promised anything to hear about my experience, and I should've taken advantage of the situation, but I hate to take advantage, besides which I only thought of it later.

"It was many years ago, when I was in college, writing the great American novel . . ."

"You call that athletic?"

"If you're going to interrupt . . . That's better . . . Anyway, I decided I needed to experience life to the fullest, and subsequently found myself at the Grand Canyon. Nothing would do but I must cross it on foot. So I climbed down, which as you doubtless know takes hours, and by that time it was getting dark. It was winter and no one else was around. In short, I got lost, and stayed lost for three icy cold days. To keep myself from freezing to death, I had to set fire to the great American novel."

Sissie shouldered her hockey stick. *"I'm* going to the field."

"I'll be along in a few minutes," I agreed, and crept with my pastry and coffee into the hibiscus.

* * *

Fielding was restitching those memoirs of Père Labat's that we'd bought in the antique shop in L-port; he set down his wooden sewing frame, pointed across sand and sea to a vague green speck in the Caribbean, and spoke feelingly of all he held dear.

"There you have the classic tragedy. Eighty-odd plantations on a single island. How can you expect to transport sugar from eighty separate mills and not go under? These small independents have destroyed free enterprise, and everyone's afraid to admit it."

"Let them grow coconuts," replied Prince Dzhusaly with a shrug, mortal toil not being his metier. The prince was attractively perched on a K'ang Hsi porcelain garden seat, from which he cast occasional profile-enhancing glances in through the French doors to the dining room, where the ladies lingered over tea. Love had come to our Sissie, in the still-youthful form of this itinerant nobleman, who pursued his languid courtship rather as a Maine fisherman phlegmatically reels in a lobster, his traps set with his archaic title and a certain limp good looks.

"Coconuts," mused Fielding, plying his needle back and forth around the heavy cords which ran up and down the sewing frame and would form the vertebrae of the volume's spine. "There must be a more viable thrust, a megacoconut." Below our piazza, servants with bare black backs and straw hats swept the immaculate gardens, while the smooth old villain above them came to the end of his thread, skillfully tied on a new piece of embroidery silk, bemoaned the failure to properly prioritize coconuts, and looked, in this radiant setting, like a little old bookbinder, with corporate slaves in seventeen countries.

In spite of a decade's dabbling in luxury, I still didn't feel altogether comfortable about servants. The islanders, it's true, quite bowled one over with their graciousness, but there was I, lolling above them and, what's more, of a paler hue.

"I can't understand Albion's time frame," muttered Fielding, indicating he wished our ship would arrive from

Maine; neither Prince Dzhusaly nor I shared his impatience. I, of course, wished to stay forever on immobile earth, and this particular spot, one must admit, was close to paradise. The prince, for his part, desired perhaps a bit more time to solidify his future before his newly beloved Sissie departed.

This fair maiden now made her appearance, striding out through the archway and causing the noble suitor to flash an incisor-sharpened smile so devoid of affection, compassion, or even physical lust, it was more obscene than a leer. A true prince, it seems, can perceive wealth at eighty-five paces, and Sissie's wealth was of infinite depth; so profound were her assets, she hadn't the foggiest idea of the figure; when she needed a large sum of money, she merely picked up the phone and told some man in an office somewhere to liquidate such-and-such amount. Dzhusaly sensed all this immediately, and sensed more, much more than I could ever see. The man was calculating beyond plebeian understanding, cold beyond mammalian freezing; in short, a prince.

"Shove over, Gregory," she ordered, joining me on a batik-cushioned banquette; I wasn't sure at the time whether her practice of cutting Prince Dzhusaly deader'n a mackerel was flirtation or simply her natural rudeness.

"Do look," cried Julia, brandishing a jeweled digit seaward.

"My camera," commanded Fielding.

We all gazed past the beach, where a black fin sliced through the water, gleaming, arrogant, deadly, and for an instant the back of the shark seemed to me like the sleeked-back black hair of Prince Dzhusaly, slicing his way through the hot afternoon to bite a mortal chunk out of Sissie's bankbook.

The fin disappeared; all was golden sunlight, white sand, green palms, showy double red-and-white bougainvillea, nature at its least savage, and the only predator in paradise was its most civilized flower, the prince, who leaned toward Sissie as if to comfort her from the shock of the sight of a shark.

"A man buys the best Nazi camera in the world and it's

never around when he needs it." Fielding was clearly put out; though Prince Dzhusaly was one of his ten thousand most intimate friends, he didn't see why the fellow had to chase after Sissie, who'd remained Miss Kingsland this long, she might as well go the rest of the voyage solo, until which time she'd leave her portfolio, interest compounded, to her young cousins, either his grandchildren or great-grandchildren, whichever way the good auditor willed it. Had he dragged the impossible girl up to Maine, bowed his silver head while she said endless grace, and flown her down to the Virgins in his private jet in order to lose his progeny's rightful legacy to the offspring of a deposed European despot?

"How elemental," sighed Julia (re the shark, or was it re Prince Dzhusaly?). I knew she couldn't agree with Fielding more; Hale blood wanted no thinning with an overbred, underenergetic, feebleminded, syphilitic (after all, who knew?), possibly hemophilic, definitely decadent, bisexual pauper.

She'd discussed it with me the day before, over tiffin (how British Empire we grew in the Virgins), quite *en confiance,* and I tended to disagree about the bisexual; I rather thought Dzhusaly asexual, but doubtless he was able to oblige in a languid way whichever gender (in eight or nine monetary digits) came his way. "Nine," Julia had murmured, showing that she knew a good deal more of Sissie's finances than Sissie; and furthermore, though she might sympathize as a woman with the poor girl's frustration, when it came down to the question of her grandchildren's money, Sissie's sexual liberation was outprioritized.

Sissie, staring resolutely out to sea while Prince Dzhusaly whispered tepid endearments, now focused her gaze more keenly on the horizon. "It's the *Potemkin.*"

Potemkin wasn't exactly the name of the yacht we all watched, but it was indeed an ex-battleship, painted an innocent springtime yellow as if to erase all memory of the many felled by its cannons; the vessel's shape, however, was impossible to change, so the main effect of the frolicking daffodil paint was to make the thing look like the gayest battleship in the Caribbean.

As this bizarre spectacle proceeded across our range of vision, we could make out the seaplane aboard, along with a launch the size of an ordinary millionaire's yacht. The crew, crisply uniformed, nonsensically numerous, made up a veritable navy, the private navy of a man whose wealth was so beyond comprehension it was (as Coco Chanel said of the Duke of Westminster) a catastrophe.

Fielding, Julia, Sissie, and I had recently spent an afternoon as guests on this floating municipality, our Arab host utterly charming and remote as Allah; I had never before understood the vast gulf between super- and merely rich, or, by way of extension, between rich and middle class, or, to carry it further, people of different race, or nationality, education, neighborhood, generation, gender and, ultimately, the unbridgeable distance between any two people in one room at any time.

We watched the gay battleship diminish and exit, stage left as it were, then before we'd finished applauding, in the wake of leviathan, a tiny white toy appeared, steering straight for our island.

"Get out your camera," said Julia to Fielding, "our ship's come."

My heart fell, along with the sunlight; dark storm clouds gathered at the horizon, where the white shape of sails imperceptibly spread and slowly divided into the unmistakable square rigging of our little bark.

The outrageously painted *Potemkin* had been ponderously impressive, but the *Hale Fellow II*, antique in design, silent, exquisite, emerged like a Turner from the turbulent storm clouds, cast toward us on slate-green waters, burnished with tradition and glory; exultation swept through us, even I ran for binoculars and, for perhaps ten overwrought seconds, caught the fever of those who "must go down to the sea."

The grizzled figure of Albion Slaggby appeared in my binoculars' lenses, beside him the equally bewhiskered individual he'd hired to accompany him on the first lap of the trip. Both wore peaked caps and oversized overalls. I felt quite emotional for dear dour old Maine.

Such sentimental rapture should always be heeded as presaging disaster.

*   *   *

Albion and his mate joined us for dinner, contributing absolute silence and that aura of dependable strength bred by inhuman winters and ice-cold fishing waters. To men of such stamp, the placid Caribbean, with its playful donkey kicks, was of nothing.

Stonily, they gummed boiled lobster, breaded turtle steaks, and crisp tania fritters, the island's answer to the potato, served in shallow baskets like nests of golden claws. Breading and butter drops fell from silent Maine lips, decorated bushy Maine beards, and embellished overall bibs. Albion and mate.

Others, however, were unusually excited. Darling Julia, who felt that the sea was about to make her a gift of her long-lost sense of youth, bubbled like the Piper Heidsieck champagne she was drinking; each effervescent burst seemed to me, wary as I was of our journey, another little bubble of nitrogen narcosis, the dread disease of divers who go too deep, which for me meant anywhere over my ankles.

The prince, also, was less lethargic than usual, seeing tonight as his last-ditch pitch for gentle Sissie's nine monetary digits. "Your skin is like the calla lily," I heard him whisper (a wildly inaccurate simile for Sissie's freckled hide) into the neck of her oxford shirt. She tittered enigmatically.

"It was Captain Bligh"—Julia gaily interrupted the prince's lovemaking, plunging her fork into the heart of her breadfruit pudding—"who brought this divine food to the islands."

I caught my unseaworthy reflection in the baroque gilded mirror which hung on the opposite wall, framed by nineteenth-century French bronze sconces. Dusky serving girls glided in and out with trays. Musicians performed outside, beneath open windows. Why, I wondered, can't we just stay put?

The coconut soufflé was exemplary and the soursop ice cream better than one would expect; I certainly didn't look forward to eating from tins for months on end.

Coffee and liqueurs dispersed us. Fielding and Albion unrolled maps and charts, along with a depressing pile of volumes in waterproof bindings listing every blue ripple from Key West to Guyana.

"Shall we go for a walk?" asked the prince of his calla lily love; his voice conveyed moonlight sonatas, island songs of passion, and the wedding march through fresh green fields of bank notes.

Julia's eyes met mine meaningfully. I could see she wished me to join her on the rose brocade, eighteenth-century canapé where we could cozily discuss the depraved royal suitor; but my heart was too heavy; I already felt the ocean's sickening roll. I excused myself and strolled out onto the veranda which encircled the house; terrazzo flooring inset with marble echoed my steps; *famille verte* vases, jardinieres, and ginger jars cast graceful shadows. I leaned over a carved balustrade, drinking the perfume of yellow thunbergia. Upstairs, my canopied bed was laid with silken sheets; the storm clouds had passed and a tropical moon shone down extravagantly; if only, I thought, there were someone here tonight to appreciate me.

I descended the stairs to the cool grass. Behind me the light from the dining room grew less insistent, and the tiled roof gleamed like fish scales. I walked toward my favorite oasis, the spot that was made for me and my appreciative someone, had that mysterious someone existed; the place was an open-walled dining pavilion with Chinese roof and skeletal beams, lacquered red, intimately sized for elegant trysts; beside this charming structure splashed a dainty waterfall, and through the pavilion's delicate form, one could see the bright sea, the white beach, and the dark silhouettes of two figures.

Who were they?

I felt something pending beneath the huge moon—a tension; the scent of blossoms was stifling and ominous. But how foolish, I thought the next moment, when one of the shadows moved, and I realized it was just sexual tension, just our own Prince Dzhusaly and Sissie, out spooning.

All around me in the woods, cicadas called to each other, along with the waterfall's music and songbirds of the night—parrots, perhaps, banana quits, or Antilles goldfinches—I was never much at identification, but I knew a bird of prey when I saw one. Prince Dzhusaly reached out a lizardlike hand and placed it rather low on Sissie's dark shape. The black figures executed a brief little dance, involving Sissie's knee—one, two, kick, to a most central part of the prince—followed by a doubling up of the royal body, a very swift fall, and equally swift exit of Sissie from the scene, her brisk athletic form crossing the stately lawn and making for the porch.

One couldn't help but reflect: Why did the wretched girl go so far as to walk with the prince in the moonlight, if only to kick him in the royal gonads?

The answer, of course, was loneliness.

If that beastly prince, at the very last moment, had presented his case with the tiniest sincerity, he might've been granted his Midas desires instead of a knee in the nuts. If there'd been one shred of something Sissie's hungry heart could respond to, she and her shares could have been his tomorrow. A solitary ray of genuine warmth—it's all any of us yearn for, would give all for—*n'est-ce pas?*

The bird of prey flailed on the sand, its black shape no longer elegantly languid, its noble beak giving voice to the most wrathful curses imaginable, ordering flaying of Sissie's body, along with feathering, beheading, drawing, quartering, and sundry other entertainments with which his enlightened ancestors had endeared themselves to their subjects. No doubt Prince Dzhusaly had experienced rebuttal before in his uncertain career, but probably had never been laid horizontal, gasping like a beached turtle.

I watched the poor turtle for some minutes, considered

going to his assistance, and decided discretion would be kinder than any dubious first aid I might render.

I moved soundlessly over the grass toward the cove, where the *Hale Fellow II* was anchored in moonlight. Her tall masts, bereft of sails, looked peculiarly ghostly. A figure lumbered on deck, Albion's mate (that lucky fellow who, no longer needed, would fly back to Maine in the morning). The calm waters splashed the hull gently, and the scene was really quite pretty, peaceful, nothing at all threatening about it—or so I told myself as I stood there shivering in the sultry evening, letting my last chance for escape slip through my fingers, gazing upon our death ship.

* * *

My intention was to spend the voyage drugged, to which end I carried on board a large supply of Dramamine, along with my personal belongings, cookbooks, and hot-water bottle.

"We'll be doing isometrics on deck each day to keep in shape," Sissie explained. Julia smiled benevolently from the dock. And Fielding came down the gangplank looking like Prince Ranier.

I tried to remain inconspicuous among my seasick pills; my principal interest was the galley, not for its gorgeous basket weave of tropical woods, purpleheart turnery, or angelique cabinets, but for the bare-bone necessities of survival—canned truffles, foie gras, caviar, vinegar aged a quarter of a century—and the tiniest of stoves with scarcely any counter room for the flailing of dough. The entire setup of this vessel distressed me, but there was nothing I could do now.

"Gregory," called Sissie, "will you help hoist the sails?"

I quickly popped into the head (condensed Louis Quinze with *chaise percée*-concealed toilet) and took a Dramamine; true, we hadn't left land yet, but Sissie's voice made me nauseous. The roar of a truck motor told me Albion had arrived back from town where he'd been shopping for steaks to put in the deep freeze.

We met in the galley.

"How's the albatross this mornin'?" he asked, glancing out to the deck where Sissie directed traffic. "She still have gravel in her beak?"

"In quantities."

He opened the freezer. "The place for a woman like that"—his voice echoed deep into cold hollow depths—"is at the nether end of a bowling alley."

6

FOR EXACTLY A MONTH WE SAILED, WITH SCARCELY a cloud, round a glittering tiara of fabulous islands, dropping anchor here and there to explore the well-known attractions. We witnessed voodoo in Haiti, danced the beguine in Martinique, snorkeled to a frazzle, and listened to steel bands until I was ready to scream; on one such occasion I happened to be seated alone in a rum shack, staring out through a bead curtain to the sea, when a tremulous old voice came at my shoulder:

"D'you know Johnny Mercer?"

I turned and looked into the eyes of the demented old millionaire. "So sorry, I don't."

Later, we visited the ancient dodo at his coral palace, where he asked Fielding, with a cackle, "Are you armed?"

Fielding replied with his virile laugh.

This confident laugh of Fielding's could've served as a model for a Carnegie course in positive thinking; hearty, unambiguous, almost dogmatic, it boomed through the boat, fore and aft, resounding plainly when under sail and at other times faintly harmonizing with the diesel engine. Albion (twice, I believe) was heard to utter a bone-dry chuckle; Julia had a wicked, throaty, gurgling giggle I adored; and Sissie basically sniggered.

What a rollicking crew we were.

Sipping Courvoisier in the boat's main saloon with its dark Georgian paneling in the evening, or basking on the gleaming teak deck beneath glorious sun and intricate rigging, we stayed resolutely amused.

"Did you ever hear," asked Sissie, "the joke about Stalin and St. Francis of Assisi . . . ?"

"I would do anything to avoid such a joke, including jump in the sea."

What I did was leap to my feet and hurriedly move mats and deck chairs, a thing we often did anyway to get out of range of Albion, who was continually cooling the deck and topsides by hosing them down with saltwater. To counteract this hosing obsession he had to rise each day at dawn and wipe the salt off the woodwork with dew. He also cleaned the entire ship, polished the brass, touched up paint and ten coats of varnish, removed doors for airing, fixed motors, flushed out the bilge, and was utterly immune to tropical heat, his only concession being removal of shirt and shoes, which left him pinkly clad in his giant bib overalls and duck-billed cap, while we pampered sailors scampered about in the skimpiest swimsuits.

I suppose I shouldn't include myself among the sailors, since I remained adamantly helpless with rope and rudder. Nor did the ship need redecorating, though I chose little things in each port to embellish Fielding and Julia's three homes; so why was I on board? In retrospect, I think it was hoped my lightness would somewhat counteract Sissie's anti-imperialist pall; in addition to which, the rich need staff around them; at the end of those mile-long driveways, on the peaks of those remote mountaintops, in their gated and blockaded compounds, where millions are spent insuring absolute privacy, the wealthy surround themselves with strangers, often with roles as vague as my own.

Family, perhaps, could serve the same equivocal purpose, but family have their own lives to lead. Fielding and Julia's children were far too busy to take off on a three-month cruise, being in the prime of their power, amassing, enlarging; nor do one's own children, middle-aged and accompanied by another generation of offspring, necessarily make one feel younger; one can't help sensing a certain counting of years till inheritance.

Instead, there was I, to hold Julia's hand (figuratively speaking), to listen to Fielding (Julia having heard his stories, Sissie too egotistical to listen, Albion unresponsive), and to help ease any little inconvenience of travel.

A-basking in the gentle sunlight, I dreamt of pears filled with chocolate souffle, and mused on friends and wine and civilized things of every kind. Dolphins leapt off the bow; there were flying fish—or some kind of fish—rising from the waves; and I walked around feeling nautical in spite of myself. Julia showed me how to do a thing with the mizzen which seemed simple and pleasant enough; I was almost learning to enjoy the rolling deck. Life at sea, I thought, is actually quite acceptable.

In bits and pieces, through these idyllic weeks as we lay on our mats on the hot teak deck, breathing the salty air, anointing each other with suntan oil, and sipping cold Carib beer, Sissie continued to nag. "Surely you've *some* interest in sailing?"

"Didn't you see my trick with the mizzen?"

"You must learn from the bottom up," she declared, determined to turn me into a sailor, possibly so I could serve in her revolutionary navy.

But her heart was well-intentioned, and if I resisted the impulse to push her overboard or stick a raw fish in her ear, it was because I feared neither action would help. She was one of those people bent on conversion—of anyone foolish enough to listen for five seconds—to her politics, morals, aerobics, diet, and religion.

"... I made a visit," she muttered; it sounded like a euphemism for a trip to the toilet, but turned out to be an elite way of saying she had walked into a church. People ramble into religious buildings for myriad reasons—architectural appreciation, *par exemple*; with Sissie, it was to belittle her fellow man.

"We Pluckroses don't much care to be converted to

anything, but like to find our own way through life, at a gentle pace if possible."

"You have no political conscience," she said. "You're the kind of person who becomes the dupe of the ideology of the masses."

"I've voted as my conscience directed," I replied pompously.

"Yes," she said in her smuggest manner, "I'm sure you did."

"Do you want me to get out with pamphlets so you can spread your confused ideas more freely?"

"I want," she said in quiet confidential tones, "to bring Fielding to his knees."

"But Sissie, the man is your host."

"He has exploited the workers of the world."

"Yes, but he has fed you, sheltered you. Isn't it callous to wish him ruin?"

"He can't really be trusted," she said mysteriously. "But Sissie, he's a Boy Scout."

I wouldn't trust Sissie to feed a chicken, and there you have it.

"What's wrong?" she asked me one morning as I sprawled on my deck chair clutching my stomach.

"I must've eaten too many Napoleons last night," I said weakly.

"Where does it hurt?"

"About here." I indicated the right side of my person.

"Bad?"

"Excruciating."

"Your appendix has burst. But don't worry, I can have it out in two hours."

"Surely you're mad," I gasped from my deck chair.

"I am anything but mad. I've got full medical supplies on board, and I was thoroughly trained in emergency surgical procedures in the Peace Corps."

"*Julia,*" I called loudly, then turning to Sissie informed her I wouldn't allow her to trim a hangnail. "*Oh, Julia . . .*"

My gracious employer presently appeared, afloat in a butterfly caftan.

"Julia," I said from my deck chair, "you must promise me you won't let Sissie operate should I be rendered unconscious."

"But Gregory, she was trained in the Peace Corps."

"Julia, please, I've merely eaten too many Napoleons."

Sissie was gazing at me like one of those female insects who bites off her husband's head. She would give me a complete examination, to my everlasting embarrassment, operate, fail, and throw me in the sea with the rest of the morning's garbage.

The pain was not subsiding, but I managed to hobble to my stateroom and lock the door.

It was at this moment, as I lay down on my narrow bed, that I first questioned Julia's sympathies. She'd seemed ready; there'd been a look in her eye; and I was on her ship.

Perhaps she was bored and thought she might enjoy nursing me back to health; perhaps, except that I would have no health at all if Sissie ever touched me.

Extraordinary girl, to think of removing my appendix.

But we Pluckroses do not surrender that quickly.

"It'll happen in our lifetime," Sissie informed me the next morning. (I am again my strong vital self, stretched out on my deck chair.) "People like Julia and Fielding will be put into factories and made to slave for every morsel they eat. Do you know how many peasants could live for a year on just one of Aunt Julia's . . . ," etc., etc.

Like her hero Fidel Castro, Sissie possessed the unusual ability to rant for five hours straight without letting anyone else get a word in edgewise. She was a dear girl, but she did carry on.

"Get out in the ghettos," she advised. "Live with the people . . ."

I lounged in my deck chair, idly perusing *Architectural Digest,* eating brandy-charged chocolate cherries, marrons glaces, and bittersweet truffles, and resting my eyes now and then on Sissie running up the mast.

"You must go into prisons," she told me. "That's where the seeds are fomenting. You must talk to the convicts and urge them to throw off their chains . . ."

This is the real life, I reflected, here in the deck chair; this is the place from which a designer can dream of forty-room mansions waiting to be tastefully furnished.

The great rooms of my imagination came and went, with Sissie's earth-shattering schemes; her sermons lapped the designs of my mind like monotonous surf; only occasionally did I actually listen, as whenever she quoted "my best girlfriend."

This bosom companion, with whom Sissie had shared adolescence and an ongoing correspondence, interested me; for years, it seemed, the blooming of an unnatural act was always on the verge between the two friends.

If only, I fantasized, gazing at the idiot's muscular thighs, I could get her to any one of a number of international watering places— which somehow she'd missed in her travels and where such flirtations were more than epistolary—

But why would I want such a thing for Sissie?

It's been a lifelong curse of mine, this fantasizing over how friends should live; it's also been a profound waste of time, particularly with someone as pedantic as Sissie, to whom nothing interesting could possibly happen.

But wait a moment. Doesn't every caterpillar come out of its cocoon eventually? Who could say our caterpillar wasn't pure silk within?

I imagined her passionate unfolding, all the prickly parts of her nature shed and the moth at last flying freely. I saw her solitude transformed into an appealing vulnerability, where each drop of loneliness she'd suffered was another aspect of her womanly worth.

Fielding, sauntering by, glanced at the girl with eyes that cared not a blink for her natural or unnatural release, but saw only, and to the precise figure, the monetary reason he had for suffering the creature aboard his ship.

"I bankrupted them in a manner of weeks," he told me tenderly, later as he sat in his deck chair, his Boy Scout sewing frame on his lap, thread slack, bronzed fingers for the moment at rest, as he stared past Sissie, out over the water, with eyes of gray steel. "They thought they could compete, and I crushed them."

The tale was repeated, with variations, changes of names, different years, but basically the same story, with the same happy ending—receivership—as we drifted along the Caribbean's Coke-bottle waters; this was, after all, my reason for being there: Fielding's Remembrance of Trusts Past.

Like a Viking of old, with large noble head, silver hair, and trails of victory, he sailed the *Hale Fellow II,* and his fond recollections grew more graphic as we got further to sea.

"I broke his back," he said softly of some long-ruined competitor. "I held him in my grip and squeezed."

Like the great horned owl, who needs to feed on three or four small mammals a day, Fielding, in his prime, needed to eat three or four small businesses, and now in his retirement, he still longed for the taste of a poor bankrupt's bones; while he reminisced, he seemed to move his well-shaped lips as if he were munching a widow's life-accumulated assets at this very moment.

When he first told me about gentlemen he'd caused to leap from tall buildings through devious business connivings and other acts of infamy, deeds which, though they didn't hang heavy on Fielding, would've destroyed anyone with a shred of human decency, I admit, my flesh crawled. I had the unpleasant suspicion that just as Sissie wanted to put Fielding in a factory, so Fielding wished to place me in one too, at slave wages, in Singapore. I had the sensation of bathing with a family of piranhas.

On the other hand, at odd little moments, sudden alterations of mood passed over my employer's countenance, and his true inner nature was almost revealed, but I was never quite fast enough to perceive it.

Fielding hadn't limited his attentions to men of business; as God's eye is on the sparrow, Fielding's was on the lowliest of workers. "You can withhold a tip from a surly waiter, but what've you taught him? The thing to do is buy the restaurant and fire the bastard." Fielding bought whatever stood in his path; he went where he wanted; at an age when other men were in rest homes, Fielding was virile as a moose.

Our tête-à-têtes showed me the tip of the mountain of his wealth, the lofty peaks of his soul, pure as arctic snow. He was impeccable and generous with me, as he'd also been, each year, to however many philanthropies his staff of tax lawyers suggested; he had contributed to most of the world's worst causes, especially in underdeveloped countries, where he'd given without stint to fight those social reformers who might've freed the serfs in his mines, fields, and factories. He could afford the magnanimous gesture; he was old, a benevolent king; he was publicly revered, above life's fights, and out of harm's way.

Albion, dumb but not deaf, took it all in as he swabbed the decks in his duck-billed cap and bib overalls. Though long Fielding's employee, he wasn't his lackey; the sea had let him preserve his independence; and if he looked at his employer with a slightly jaundiced eye, he still maintained his integrity because he was of the elements. (Fielding's element was a long conference table of French-polished mahogany, set with cigars, maps, and Rolaids, at which the competition was liquidated.)

"You have to understand him," explained Julia; we sat in her stateroom, a bit of Versailles miniaturized to fit between bulkheads. The built-in bed was flanked by satin-brocaded fauteuils; I perched on one, while Julia primped at her Lalique-and-Baccarat-cluttered collapsible poudreuse.

I don't wish to conjure up images of monkeys' things and goat glands, but there was an aura of sad rejuvenation about Julia at this time. Like an aging movie queen in search of a new starring vehicle, she sashayed through that month afloat with desperate brilliance, and if, like the old movie queen, her dance steps had to be choreographed around a convenient deck chair (or fauteuil), nonetheless, she still looked lovely surrounded by Lalique and Baccarat.

"So many of my friends rely on Scotch tape." She studied her face in the glass, and found her tawny skin—praise be—

still relatively taut at the cheekbones. "As soon as they start fluffing their hair forward, I know. But with all this salt and humidity . . . dear Dr. Levinson . . ." Her conversation was often elliptical. "Promise me, Gregory, you won't start lifting before you need it. Such a tragedy, to begin too early, and then live on and on when there's no more to work with . . . poor dear Clare . . ." She rattled on, assuming forced gaiety. (Sometimes it seemed to me, when she stood on deck staring at the horizon, that she might be considering a leap.)

A knock at the door ushered in our host, her husband, my boss, the empire builder indulging in simple pleasures— something like our president watching football on TV. He wore silk slacks and a gay batik shirt, and his invincibility, the triumphs of seventy years, shone from every bronzed pore, each pearly manicured nail as he offered his wife's coiffure a pat. "Remember Binkie?" he asked.

"Yes, why?" she replied.

"I was just thinking about him."

Julia glanced my way in her mirror. "Fielding purchased Binkie's company several years back."

After which, one assumes, Binkie plunged from the nearest high building. It was difficult to accept that at this very instant Fielding was grinding people to bits, in boardrooms all over the earth, while I was floating around in his rococo bathtub, the recipient of his considerable charm, most intimate reminiscences, an eighteen-karat Piaget watch, and some very fine primitive paintings I'd admired in Haiti.

This simple boat, this simple sea, this simple evening— here was the goal of Fielding's life, its summation, a man's simple dream— was it so much to ask? It seemed, in fact, very little, in exchange for fifty years of crushing competitors: To float along with one's aging wife, one's disagreeable niece, one's decorator, and one toothless old salt, it wasn't really a very great deal.

Perhaps if all the poor souls Fielding had ruined could see the humble result of their sacrifice, they wouldn't feel so bitter. If they could hear him mellifluously reading *Great Expectations* as they drifted to sleep . . . Even Sissie had grown to enjoy our bedtime readings, it was the only time she looked peaceful.

I left the man with his dream, and climbed to the deck, thinking, I'm really enjoying my little talks with Fielding. It's all quite harmless. Nothing serious rides on anything Fielding says or Julia does.

I'm free to enjoy life.

I've found a good berth.

In the silvery moonlight, our grizzled skipper, steering our tall ship by the stars, looked exactly like Captain Ahab, with pale floating beard in the wind, bib overalls blowing, body hard as the shell of a geriatric crab, and that profile carved out of New England granite.

"Evening," I said respectfully, aware I was addressing not merely Albion, but also Ishmael, Queequeg, and an entire tradition of seafaring heroes.

Albion didn't respond.

"How are you tonight?" I persisted.

He said not a word.

I continued: "The water's almost phosphorescent."

If Albion agreed, he kept quiet about it.

"And," I elaborated, "the air's unusually balmy."

This comment stirred no controversy.

Encouraged, I grew more personal: "Tell me, Albion, have you been a navigator all your life?"

Following this brilliant conversation, we fell into silence, or I fell into silence and Albion deeper into tradition.

"Gregory," fluted a voice from the companionway, the voice of she who hounded me by day and by night. Her pug features gleamed in the moonlight as she strode with determination to where I stood by the skipper. "I wonder if I could ask you to take some dictation."

"Why? Are you formulating a new world plan?"

"My thoughts move so fast," she replied, "my fingers can't keep up."

"That's what tape recorders are for," I retorted.

"But I like the living ear." It sounded vaguely obscene.

I removed my pen from my pocket and showed her, by

the glow of the moon, how I held my writing instrument with thumb locked under forefinger in a manner making swift shorthand impossible. "So you see, there's not much I can do to help."

She wandered off in a sort of dream, her world manifesto stewing in her brain. At the very next port, I decided, I'll buy a large hat and some earplugs, effectively blocking out both sight and sound of the woman.

"That's a fierce turkey," muttered Albion. "You wanna watch her when she gobbles."

"So long as she doesn't gobble me."

He gazed out from under beaked cap. "Mebbe."

"She's got a lot on her mind," I sighed.

"Boils down to ruttin'."

"I beg your pardon."

"There's need for a bull in her barnyard."

I thought of the prince, who'd been felled practically in his own barnyard. "I don't know, Albion."

"Yessir." He tugged at his cap. "I seen it many times." Then in a different tone, reminiscent of mad Captain Ahab: "I advise you to watch the moon."

With jutting beak, nose, and beard, he stared at that unfathomable orb and glittering firmament, and his piercing sea gaze seemed to dare wind and weather to throw him their worst.

As yet, I'd managed to avoid humiliation in squalls, storms, or buckets, so standing there seeing our captain challenge the elements, I thought, *Please, Albion, don't ask for too much.*

But the old mariner's perverse prayer was answered.

More fully than even he could have wanted.

7

"I'M COMING TO LIKE FIELDING," I TOLD SISSIE.
"He really is a brick underneath, once you get to know him."

"How dense you are."

"Oh, he's gruff at times, and impatient at others, but I feel his genuine affection for me and how it has grown."

We were arguing in the galley, where I was chilling some cucumber soup and whipping up a mixed-seafood quiche. I'm not by any stretch of the imagination a great cook, but I manage a few things adequately: a sprig of mint in ice-cold soup, well-seasoned eggs done a dozen ways, the honest taste of carrots laced with butter-brown pistachios and Cointreau, and the simplest *salade verte*.

"Yes," I said to Sissie, "I've come to occupy a place in Fielding's life that goes beyond being an employee. I believe he looks upon me as a nephew, or something closer. I understand the great man's cares and woes. A bond is being formed that will last a long time, that will stand me well in some future hour. I can tell . . . And now will you kindly clear out, and let me serve?"

The dining room was my favorite room, filled with flowers I amassed in each port, A velvet-tufted banquette made a half-moon round the Adam table, which, along with the sideboard and silver wine cooler, was bolted to the floor. There was a feeling of ultimate safety; no adversity could rock us or shake us, with everything so handsome and so firmly bolted.

Candelabra blazed on white damask and an azure Art

Nouveau service swirled with ivory, peach, and black tulips; the sterling was a heavy shell-and-thread from some stalwart ancestor; our tanned faces and hands, burnished more gold still by the flickering candles, looked strangely Egyptian; I had a fanciful notion, that fateful evening, that our ship was the pharaoh's solar bark.

"Gregory," said Julia, "that was an excellent quiche."

Fielding dabbed at his lips with a napkin. "There once was a murderer . . ." he said thoughtfully.

I paused, goblet in hand, wondering whether he was about to describe a business partner.

"... When Mount Pelee erupted, he was locked in a thick-walled cell. Of a population of thirty thousand he was the only one to survive the molten lava."

"Which shows," said Sissie, "he was the only honest man in the village."

"What it shows," said Fielding, "is the importance of being firmly entrenched, especially in times of economic uncertainty."

I drained my Bailey's Irish Cream to the dregs and teetered out onto the deck to take my turn at the helm.

Albion greeted me with his usual muteness, to which I replied: "Cucumber soup and quiche. I put your piece in the warming oven."

In response the old sailor lumbered away, and I was alone.

By this time I could be trusted with simple nautical chores, namely gazing at the sea on placid evenings, long enough for Albion to eat.

It worked out well, because I usually needed a breath of fresh after dinner, I loved the tropical twilight deeply, and it made a change for the others. I admit it fed my landlubber's ego, feeling the *Hale Fellow II* in my hands—though of course if anything really boaty were required, they wouldn't have left it to me.

It would be an interesting study, *je pense,* to find out exactly what occurs in people's minds the moment before catastrophe. Bonaparte, for example at Waterloo. Ah well, it's doubtless been done. But at that pivotal instant of the

Hale Fellow II's destiny, I'm pleased to report my thoughts weren't trivial in the least; I looked on life and saw it was good.

A chain of islands lay in the distance, but there was little wind, our craft moved slowly, and I calculated Albion would be back on deck before we'd get close enough to any land mass to require real steering. It has been said of these Caribbeans that when King Ferdinand asked Columbus to describe them, the explorer crumpled a piece of parchment and tossed it onto the table; but not all the islands are convoluted and mountainous; the chain that lay before us was rather like a flat string of beads, it's only intricacy being a network of deeply cut coves.

Out of one of these coves, in the glimmering dusk, a small motorboat appeared. It was a cabin cruiser, the sort one sees by the hundreds in every harbor of the Antilles, and I thought nothing of it; after all, they could see our large craft, and there was still plenty of distance, but the distance rapidly narrowed, and they seemed to be bearing directly for us.

They're drunk, I thought, and will wait until the last minute to swerve; this had happened before, but it always annoyed me, and tonight, alone with the ship in my care, I found it disturbing; not alarming, mind you, but definitely disturbing.

The stars weren't yet shimmering, just the first had come out; for some reason I thought it was Venus. A uniform gray blanketed water and sky, with the string of islands quite black upon the horizon, like jet necklaces worn by Victorian widows.

Above the roar of the cruiser's motor came the sound of its hull slapping the waves; as the drunken boat made for the *Hale Fellow II,* its features zoomed suddenly clear. Several men were working swiftly (and utterly soberly) on deck, maneuvering a piece of machinery under a large tarpaulin. Whatever can that be? I wondered.

The vessel bore down, the tarp was stripped back, and I was staring into the nostrils of heavy artillery.

Bravery has never been my strong suit; to tell you the truth, cowardice is as integral a part of my nature as blue eyes or a fondness for chocolate. As the machine gun started to fire, I saw my whole precious life pass in vibrant hues before me.

I saw great rooms I have done: A marquetry forest draped its delicate rosewood foliage around two Louis Seize daybeds, over the doorframe, and on out to the atrium. Smoke mirrors were pierced by illuminated windows containing gold Buddhas. A swan-shaped tub, a dolphinesque sink, and a harp were harmoniously grouped in a basic black bath-sitter. There were vases containing a hundred perfect white roses; rare Louis Quatorze chandeliers; priceless Flemish paintings. I saw, I judged, and I found it wanting.

Great restaurants passed in review, and great meals. In that terrible split second of time, I dined in every three-star restaurant of Europe, as well as the four noble restaurants of New York. I ate, I drank, I chatted with good company; and it wasn't enough.

But what more is there? I wondered, and then before me paraded my loves; Vivaldi played in the background. (This was, I admit, a frightfully long minute.) One after another they appeared, with tender eyes and smooth naked limbs, and I saw—I'd loved often, I'd loved passionately, but not well.

While all this was occurring, *naturellement*, I was directly in line of fire; I would like to be able to say I fought back, called for help, or at least was wounded with dignity. Just as the lovers, the great coqs-au-vin, and trompe l'oeil marble cornices were floating before me, several bullets meant for my heart whizzed instead past my ear as I fell into a swoon.

Having hit the deck, I remained there, groveling in the most abject fright. My cowardice had saved me this far, but I felt certain death was near. Have you ever been in an accident, or barely missed one? You know how you feel when your car approaches that ditch? You feel, *This is it*. And—unless you're one of those rare souls of iron—ten to one, you barter.

Lord, I dribbled to the deck, as the attack boat landed

beside us and its machine gunners climbed heavily aboard, *I will change my worthless ways.*

If only you get me through this one, I promised, I will be a different person. You won't recognize me. I will forsake all golden Buddhas, no matter how effective they look with smoke mirrors; I will eat only in cafeterias and juice bars; I will love not for charm or for beauty, but rather the poor and the needy, the halt and the lame; I will serve not the rich, but the angels. (Here, I must say, I was picturing angels of Florentined plaster, festooning the headboard of a Renaissance bed.)

Noisily charging the companionway, one of the murderous crew paused to lift me by the scruff of my new batik and dragged me along with the group. *Quelle* group. They were uniformly ugly— or so it seemed at first blush—filthy, smelly, evil, hairy, and lacking in those early advantages that come to mean so much later on; the average age appeared to be fifty, so there wasn't much hope of reorienting their life goals and values.

We clattered into the main saloon, which showed signs of hasty abandonment, then made a rush for the radio room, where huddled my fellow passengers. Fielding sat frantically working the signal controls, and the others had the appearance of three roasted quail *en croûte,* garnished with green grapes, Madeira sauce, and a pûté of their own livers.

The gentleman who'd been yanking my batik let go his choke hold and went for Fielding, or more specifically, the radio equipment, with raised submachine gun.

"*El stupido,*" snapped one of the others. "That's a hundred thousand dollars' worth of equipment. Disconnect it, don't destroy it."

I eyed the beast who'd just spoken, and realized: It's the ship they want; we're extraneous. And my sinking hope fell five or six fathoms deeper into the sea. If only, I thought, gazing at the faces of my helpless companions and our trigger-happy captors, I'd listened to the voodoo priestess in Haiti who warned me about this.

"You will meet with adventure," she'd predicted in portentous patois as she pointed to the anchored *Hale Fellow II.*

And I'd said to myself, That's the kind of crap they hand all the tourists.

If only I'd understood.

My eyes sought darling Julia for solace; but Julia's brilliance had fled. Before me stood a dizzy old lady who'd always relied on her servants, husband, and plastic surgeon, and even now felt she'd be taken care of, just as soon as this silly misunderstanding was unraveled.

Poor fool, I thought, and turned to Sissie, for spiritual guidance. She was gazing at our captors with her most arrogant smile of contempt; the Pope and the Party, said her manner, would win in the end. I would've liked to drown her; what must our captors have felt?

My eyes met those of our captain. As I think I've indicated, the relationship between myself and Albion was not a close one; I'd held two conversations with the man between here and August. But in this hideous moment in the radio room, a bond was being forged—the bond of realism, deeper than blood. Above the old salt's whiskers, beneath his peaked cap, his bloodshot sea eyes saw the truth; and truth, for Albion, was the plank.

"What're we waiting for?" grumbled one of the assassins, jabbing me (quite unnecessarily) in the batik with his gun. We were pushed and prodded out of the cabin. Our hosts were not men of great patience, and plainly saw no lasting benefit to be derived from entertaining five perfect strangers with whom they had little in common.

Fielding, beneath the strain, was babbling jibberish to the leader, who wasn't less murderous-looking than the others but had fewer black gaps in his leer (which is always such an advantage) and his single good eye wore a calculating glint. So Fielding had pounced on this great mind of the group and was bending his hairy ear with incoherent pleas for mercy.

While I watched this painful scene, my employer paused

for an intake of breath, met my glance, and looked me over thoroughly, as if considering my worth as a human sacrifice, then rightly decided I had none.

It did seem terribly unfair that I should lose my relatively young and pure life simply because I'd linked my destiny to Fielding's. After all, he'd been asking for it, riding around in this baroque gondola, flaunting his dividends.

And then I seemed to recall a vague telepathic feeling I'd had in every port—a sensation of being followed. It'd been especially vivid when purchasing baskets.

The grapevine linking the islands had spotted us, marked us, and doomed us, and why? Because of Fielding's ostentation. In this day and age it suddenly appeared to me the worst possible taste to cruise in opulence among the poor of the world.

Listen, I wanted to tell the brigands, this isn't my show. It's his. I'm just the fellow who makes the cucumber soup.

Beside the ship in the moonlight a porpoise swam freely. I wished I were a porpoise. Nobody resents porpoises. How lucky to be a porpoise.

How lucky to be anything and anywhere other than what and where I now was. I'd give my very soul to be in Houston, spreading artistic refinement among Fuffie Blunt's impossible friends; why had I been such a snob? Houston, Houston, it sounded like heaven.

A gentleman with a scar of pure *violette de Parme* meandering from temple to temple and suggesting a recent lobotomy relieved his mental tension by incessantly clicking the safety on his heavy artillery.

Would that I could return to the very worst place I'd ever lived, the lowest ebb of my life until now, an unutterably seedy, toilet-in-the-hall, cold-water, three-cubicle walk-through on Avenue D, where I was bitten on the toe by a roach. What ecstasy, to be bitten by a roach on Avenue D, and have years, and not moments, of life ahead of me.

Another gentleman of the party, jowls dripping with evil, gave me a friendly nudge that shook my late mixed-seafood quiche to rennet.

Dear God, I'd rather be a vacuum cleaner salesman than in the position I now find myself. How cheerfully I would trudge up long flights of tenement stairs, offering time-payment cleanliness to women in curlers.

Where did I go wrong?

Is it early or late in one's youth that one makes the decision: I will be a vacuum cleaner salesman.

My own choice seemed to have been made in utero. Nowhere in my entire infancy, childhood, or maturity had the possibility occurred to me. And yet it was so obvious. Whoever heard of a vacuum cleaner salesman walking the plank?

Throughout this retrospective crisis of career, I continued being prodded and pushed, but gradually I noticed our captors' impatience had slackened.

Fielding's babbling seemed to be getting to them.

Fielding's babbling, I now perceived, was not idle delirium.

Fielding F. Hale, on the dark deck of the *Hale Fellow II*, with six submachine guns pointed in his general direction, was conducting a meeting of the board.

Because Fielding, *au fond*, was a Boy Scout. He'd gotten his merit badge in survival, and survival, for Fielding, meant money.

". . . a little in-depth communication. So you've assumed a new piece of equity. But how much product can you move in a seventy-two-foot bark? You're still at phase zero, think-tanking. What you've got here is leverage—not just seventy-two feet of capital-loss liability, but an innovative interface. The bark plus ten million for each . . . myself, my wife, and my niece."

I sensed his counting of noses was casual, and wished to remind him of the Boy Scout oath, which I felt sure contained some clause about never deserting your decorator.

The thing to do was offer an additional ten million for self and friend Albion, but I couldn't think of anyone who'd give ten dollars for either of us; *au contraire*, I suddenly recalled several—smooth-limbed ships in the night—who would cheerfully contribute fifty cents each to the kitty to hear my poor body had been lost at sea. Albion, perhaps, might rate slightly higher; I assumed his wife, if he had one, considered such a silent mate unobjectionable. But ten million dollars, I felt sure, was wildly beyond the well-meaning capacity of every far-flung relation and neighbor of Albion's on the north coast, if they held fund-raising bean suppers, pot lucks, and bingo games nightly for a month, or forever.

The meeting of the board, however, had given food for thought.

We were not to be immediately disposed of, but were tied rather tightly together, wrist to wrist, I between Julia and Sissie, and bundled aboard the cabin cruiser.

Julia's inability to grasp reality I found faintly touching, but Sissie was rather a shock; the dreadful girl seemed to have shed her highest political ideals and reverted to caste with the speed of an epileptic chameleon.

"I don't know what's become of the Caribbean," she drawled loudly, as if the whole sea were a first-class hotel in which an abominable mistake had been made and some lower-class workers been given a room.

"I *will* complain to the consulate," she added, as one might threaten to talk to the management about slipshod service, perhaps a lack of warm towels; everything would shortly be set right, said her tone, but unfortunately one must wait a few moments, as when the electricity goes out in a storm. She turned to a gentleman whose pock-marked face was permanently etched with a passion for sadism and ritual murder. (In my experience at romantic watering places, I've seen people play at sadism; this man was decidedly not a player, but a professional.)

"D'you know who we are?" she asked him.

He glanced at her with awakened interest, lifted the barrel of his gun, and touched it to her forehead. "Shut up."

The imperious idiot continued her fuming, though rather more quietly, addressing her haughty complaints mainly to me, as if I must surely understand and agree. While I didn't agree, I understood completely, and was terror-stricken enough for both of us.

Julia leaned over my quivering shape and whispered to her niece, "I don't think, dear, we ought to address them as servants. Latin men tend to be terribly proud. Last time we were in Acapulco, our maître d' . . ."

An incomprehensible story ensued, involving a tourist show at a brothel, a donkey, and a great deal of flowers, while our craft cut through the star-spangled water where lazy turtles swam without a care in their homely little heads.

And then, immediately in the wake of the lazy turtles, from the inky depths of the soup, rose a shark's fin.

It was in this instant, with Julia's inane donkey saga twittering at one ear and Sissie's tactless complaints to the management battering the other, that I had my premonition.

I would never see civilization again.

I would be quartered in old pirate style with oakum ablaze in my mouth like Luchow's *Kaiserschmarren.*

And each year, on the anniversary of my death, the wraith of the *Hale Fellow II* would appear to men and women of taste everywhere who happened to be near a body of water— East River or Hudson, the Hamptons or Fire Island, Cap Ferrat, Capri, or the Costa del Sol—a ghost ship to haunt and remind them of my early demise.

I fell into ceaseless prayer and resolution. With a sob I offered my all to the gods who protect innocent decorators.

The passionate cry seemed to vanish at once.

I was lost on a boundless sea, a dumb witness to my own tragedy.

The charm of tropical islands, I must say at this point, was rapidly fading.

8

Don't talk to me about mosquitoes.

We were bound hand and foot, and tossed unceremoniously into a quaint, Paul Gauguin sort of hut picturesquely thatched with banana leaves.

Mosquitoes, poisonous centipedes, boa constrictors, iguanas, black widow spiders, tarantulas, and rats riddled with typhoid fleas joined us for the evening.

To be taken prisoner is a ghastly thing.

Each of us has dreamed of the knock in the night, the cold face of authority, the clanging of bars behind us; it's bred in our psyche every year around income-tax time.

All the while we were on the cabin cruiser heading for our prison, I'd deceived myself into believing I understood my predicament, but it wasn't actually until they tossed me into that hut like a slave, like a dog, like a used piece of Kleenex, that stark lucidity gripped me.

Humanity no longer prevailed, because these men didn't consider us human; communication was unthinkable, compassion out of the question; one could only hope for a minimum of gratuitous cruelty before execution.

Dropping to the floor of the hut, I fell into convulsive and uncontrollable shivering. Here was life before grace, survival of the fittest, dinosaurs and pterodactyls, and I didn't stand a hothouse daisy of a chance.

I wept.

I ground my teeth, ruining the bridgework that had kept my dentist in gold necklaces for years.

"Are you all right, dear?" came a voice from the darkness; though treated with marked absence of real etiquette, in fact, on the contrary, tossed in a hut and bound, Julia was still luncheon hostess, inquiring if my tea needed hottening.

In lieu of response, I underwent a series of heart palpitations; blood vessels rang in my ears.

Sissie's voice spoke up, a few feet from the ringing. "I'll see them hanged." It was quite a natural Charles Laughton imitation. "Scum," she added with audible spittle.

"Don't you think that's severe?" asked Julia. "I've decided, when the time comes, I'm going to ask that they be rehabilitated. You can see they've had no advantages. They've probably suffered in the most backward Latin American jails."

"It's that namby-pamby, do-good, liberal attitude that's allowed such people to exist," countered Sissie. "Their parents should've been sterilized at birth."

A political dialogue ensued, with Julia prattling in her harebrained way and Sissie indignantly calling for peon blood; but basically, they agreed; everything would be straightened out in due course, by Fielding, or Sissie's trustees, or the Daughters of the American Revolution.

People who lead ivory tower lives, it seems, have difficulty seeing plain facts, the facts in this case being that we were all going to be boiled à la langouste and served without so much as a creative sauce.

The smell in the hut was disgusting. Had someone relieved themselves on the floor? Had I? In horror, I recalled the poor mountain gorilla, who senses his coming demise as a race and barely bothers to mate anymore or to leave his nest when he defecates. We were back to nature, and it was obnoxious—heat of 120 degrees, without wash water, without deodorant, without hope. Our gruesome end. I felt like a stuffed nature exhibit entitled *The Squalid Conditions of a Dying Species*.

"I wonder where they've got Fielding," mused Julia.

Wherever it was, I felt sure, there were screens, air-conditioning, and a long conference table.

"Shall we play a game?" she suggested. "Twenty questions?"

From the steaming blackness, in the direction of my left foot, came the dour tones of Albion. "It'd be more fitten if we prayed."

"Nonsense," snapped Sissie, naturally assuming it was she he'd addressed, as prayer director. Her refusal relieved me no end, but surprised me as well; here was the opportunity of her career—and probably her last—with congregation bound hand and foot. "To think of those loathsome creatures treating us as if we were no more than . . ."

". . . piss holes in the snow," supplied Albion in Old Testament tones. Now that our captain's silence had been broken, was he going to turn out to be a revivalist? I entertained the most sickening image of us going to our death singing "Rock of Ages," in four-part harmony, with Albion's woeful Presbyterian bass keeping the beat.

"Albion," I cried, clutching at the last ebb of my life force, "you know all about knots. Maybe you can untie us."

Our captain was the salt of the earth, but his mind worked slowly. I sensed his dour gray matter churning over my bleating suggestion, but, in the end, all that issued was, "We been clove-hitched."

I took this to mean he wasn't up to playing Houdini, but at least my idea had distracted him from hymns and, perhaps, since death was inevitable, that was the great thing. If men and women of taste everywhere were to be reminded of my tragic demise via annual ghost ships, I'd hate to have the effect destroyed by a vulgar choir on the soundtrack.

The mosquitoes, at this point, must have addled my brain, because again I clutched at visions of freedom. How I would get free was irrelevant, but the mirage persisted:

I was Robinson Crusoe . . . marooned on his desert island . . . bearded, bronzed, and ready to cope like an Englishman.

Except I wasn't an Englishman; there was no way for such as myself to survive on an island sans Calphalon fry pans, *herbes de Provence,* or a subscription to *House & Garden.*

Besides, I wasn't going to be given the chance to try.

Existential alienation set in, and I resumed my palpitations.

Have you ever wakened from a nameless nightmare, awash in cosmic loneliness, and thought, This is what death will be? Almost instantly, you cling to your pillow, or switch on the comforting light, or get up and go to the bathroom; you might turn on the television; in any event, you crowd out that horrible truth, that hollow glimpse of the earth's complete indifference to you.

I knew I wasn't Robinson Crusoe, but neither was I Gregory Pluckrose. Gregory Pluckrose, with his glib combinations of Regency faux-bamboo chairs and Braque lithographs, his bold blending of botanical prints and neon-winged ceilings—what had that delightful dream called Gregory Pluckrose to do with this sweating, shivering, itching, miserable body huddled in a dark stinking hut, in a bug-ridden jungle, in chains, and possibly excrement.

As you can see, in a mere matter of hours, my health was wrecked, my spirit broken, my sanity jeopardized, and my bridge-work endangered.

Memory of that first day is muddled; I must've been feverish much of the time, because my next clear recollection is of the following night.

The clove hitches at our feet were untied, and we were again marched, at gunpoint, aboard the cabin cruiser; the cove was dark and the *Hale Fellow II* nowhere in sight.

Fielding looked ghastly. Had his negotiations failed? In the dim glow of the deck lamps, his ruddy face was drained like one of those penny wax bottles of bright-colored syrup, sucked gray.

When we'd got clear of the cove, our captors switched out all lights and navigated blind; this seemed particularly ominous; it's a comfort to know where one is, even if where one is happens to be the site of one's imminent grave in the great *bouillabaisse*.

Conversation lacked sparkle.

No one had slept the previous night, nor did submachine guns tickling one's ribs inspire light give-and-take. My own contribution was limited to a rhythmic dental chattering—

tick-tock, tock-tick, ticka-tock-tock—like a Timex whose warranty has run out.

The bandits spoke to each other mostly in Spanish, with an English word occasionally thrown in as on Puerto Rican television. Their gruff voices and hulking shapes personified machismo, a mystique that charms from a distance but tends, I decided, to pale at close quarters.

For some reason, of all the shadowy faces on the deck of the cruiser that night, the one which stays most in my mind is the grizzled visage of Albion: motionless, mute, morose, yet strangely serene, lost in memory of a long life rapidly drawing to its close. *Here as anywhere,* his beady eyes seemed to say, and maybe he'd said it so many times, on numerous North Atlantic swells, in surprise winter storms off Maine, in typhoons and gales from here to frigid Fundy, that his soul had a sort of well-rehearsed farewell routine worked out.

Our captors appeared uncommonly fussy over where to sink our bodies; we puttered along through the ocean for several hours, until gradually the boat's motor came to a stop, and land loomed darkly.

Where there is life, it is said, there is hope. One might equally note, where life persists, so does terror. I wished the whole thing were over and done; if I must become a shark's dinner-for-one, so be it, but why shunt me from one sinister spot to another, torturing my fevered imagination with a dozen fates worse than death?

A long narrow harbor welcomed us like the jaws of a crocodile. Our boat slipped into the cove toward the beach, where two figures waited with lanterns.

A well-aimed shove with the snout of a gun is quite as eloquent as words; we were directed along a path through dense forest, whose vegetation seemed hostile, brushing our faces with cloying dampness, clicking with night-feeding insects; the heat was stifling, the air was menacing, the place despised us on sight, or on principle.

The path wound on for a mile, until blocked by the caterpillar canvas of a military supply truck. We were piled into the back, where we squatted opposite our guards like so many brood hens; then our pilgrimage continued, the vehicle bouncing, ascending, up into the island's mountainous interior.

The back of the supply truck was fairly dark, but I could make out—opposite, me—the chiseled features of a young man, his eyes half closed in profound contemplation; scarcely lifting his sleepy lids, he thrust out a muscular hand, grabbed my wrist, wrenched off my new eighteen-karat Piaget, and resumed his inner star gazing. The whole assault happened so fast, I barely had time to react, but did so a second later; lightning pains zigzagged down my arm, a delicate anemonelike opening and closing manifested in my chest, the tintinnabulation of bells, bells, bells musically pealed, and I experienced another discreet but poignant intimation of coronary thrombosis.

Like Queen Victoria, I was not amused. This was not my idea of adventure. My idea of adventure, basically, was a croissant. Flaky and fresh with a large *café crème*. That was my idea of adventure. The difficulty I found myself in was all very well for Errol Flynn, who apparently thrived on pirates, but Gregory Pluckrose did not.

My interest in the commercial endeavors of our hosts was similarly slight. Whatever illegal contraband they needed yachts for was strictly their business, as long as it didn't involve white slaves of both sexes oeing shipped out to Hong Kong and forced to bead cardigans.

Each stage of our transportation sharpened one's impression that this was hardly a fly-by-night outfit, a view confirmed by our destination: Cut into the jungle stood a compound as heavily guarded as any private residential community in Southern California.

Exclusive!Prestigious!   Secluded!Surrounded   by Nature!Hard to believe you 're only minutes from the San Diego Freeway! Visit soon with your architect. Fielding was visiting with his designer, wife, niece, and Albion—that's how impressed he was.

The glimpse I got of the main buildings, as they piled us

out of the truck and herded us along, wasn't exactly Old Bel Air, but the feeling was impregnable, permanent, and decidedly dampening to any fantasies one might harbor of being rescued by bugle-blowing cavalry.

The houses didn't hunch in the dirt, but sat on stilts, with real doors, real windows, and real guard dogs, eyes glinting as they prowled the moonlight.

The guest cottage, by way of contrast—some hundred yards from the compound—was strikingly like the one we'd just come from, except the interior was furnished with a central post of iron, from which hung four heavy chains— one each for Julia, Sissie, Albion, and myself. Apparently, Fielding was to be kept with our captors, which still gave a soupcon of hope; that is what I told myself as my hands were untied and my ankle chained to the post.

In darkness they left us—four famished captives; only cracks in the bamboo wall allowed night to enter, along with a swarm of mosquitoes. If those bamboo walls could've held scrawls, I felt they would have read, *Here I died, feverish . . . the rest of the message trailing off in blood.

There was no question it had been used as a prison before, a veritable death row. My persona was fast sliding into the mire; one couldn't keep up appearances chained to a stake. I felt filthy and irritable and was painfully reminded of a savage game played by neighborhood children long ago; who was tied to the stake, I couldn't quite recall, but I suspected it was little Pluckrose.

Could one have faith in Fielding?

The prospect in that corner seemed grim.

The best one really could hope for was a quick clonk on the head.

Across from me in the darkness crouched the stubborn shape of Sissie, her pug-nosed breathing labored with fury and the stultifying heat.

It was absolutely the worst spot a decorator could find himself in. What can you do with a dirt floor and a stake? What arrangements can you make with only a chain for ornament? A heavy chain at that. One felt quite like an anchor. One felt rotten.

With nothing to inspire the creative mind, I would probably just go to pieces. Perhaps I'd already gone there. What a peculiar turn of fate for a gentle art consultant. What a rude interruption.

"Gregory," announced Julia in a strained lively voice, "as soon as this bit of bother is cleared up, we're going on a nice little antique excursion. You'll like that, won't you, dear?"

"Yes, Julia," I assured her.

"We'll go abroad," she babbled, "and attend the auctions in Europe, they're such fun the auctions in Europe, so amusing . . ." she giddily explained to the darkness, her patrician pronunciation floundering, falling into that semi-British confusion of senile American dowagers. "D'you know Bonhams in Knightsbridge?" she asked me gaily.

"Yes, Julia," I said softly, almost forgetting my own misery in pity for the poor darling; it might've been my own mother in chains. How cruel that life should deal a woman such a blow at her age.

"Gregory," she asked, "when are they bringing our tea?"

"Soon," I said soothingly, inwardly raging against our captors, who would take a delicate creature like Julia and reduce her to prattling in a shack about Bonhams; I feared she was the first casualty among us, lost to hopelessness and terror.

The door pushed open, a lantern appeared, and a large wooden bowl of something unsavory and a pitcher of liquid were shoved into our midst.

"I'd like some jam with my tea," said Julia brightly.

The door was slammed in her face.

"Thank you so much," she murmured graciously, then turned to me: "Servants aren't what they once were."

"For God's sake, Julia," said Sissie, "shape up."

"How can you be so unfeeling?" I whispered to Sissie. "Can't you see how your aunt is suffering?"

"Oh, Gregory," moaned Julia, "I'm so unhappy."

"I will help you," I vowed, groping for the food in the dark, and encountering Albion's hard hand.

"As the feller says," he remarked, shoving a fistful of the stuff between his lips, "we'll soon be hangin' our boots up."

Having thus given his morbid opinion, he gummed his last meal loudly; I did likewise. It was boiled God-knows-what, soggy and glutinous, but I devoured it like a mad dog; Pluckrose, I thought— appalled, but somewhat admiring— you are at last getting down to the basics of life.

"What is it?" asked Julia.

"Boiled owl," replied our skipper.

"Perhaps I'll pass," she sighed. "I've been meaning to go on the Scarsdale Diet." Scarsdale Diet indeed, I thought, complete with pending bullet through heart.

But boiled owl? Had Albion lied, wanting more for himself? It was dreadful to believe he'd be so selfish; I preferred to believe he sincerely thought it was boiled owl . . . and sincerely hoped it wasn't.

The pitcher contained lukewarm water, doubtless writhing with amoebae, but I slugged it down like young spring Beaujolais, then passed it politely to Sissie, who kicked it away. Were both women camels? Before they could change their minds, I helped myself to their portions. Getting *far* down to basics, I thought, listening to my bestial slurping and Albion's greedy gumming of boiled whatever. The feminine temperament, I mused, pigging out in the dark while our women starved, is definitely finer.

"I'll have them gassed," declared Sissie. "The governor of California's a personal friend."

"I feel sorry for the poor things," replied Julia. "Latin America's such a harsh place, isn't it, dear? You know much more about it than I do, the wretched masses, the oppressed, the downtrodden . . ."

I thought to myself that Fielding had trodden on any number of them personally, but this didn't occur to his wife. "I feel such empathy," she continued. "Especially those two younger ones . . . did you notice the boy with the rather chiseled features? They've had so little opportunity in life, and such a chance, so strong and unspoiled . . ."

Is she, I wondered, going to hire them as chauffeur and gardener? The one with the chiseled profile would look superb in a Bentley; he had such a natural feeling for elegance, as shown by his taste in watches. Maybe she'd also hire one of the older downtrodden masses to help on the boat; they were outstanding sailors, though admittedly poor hosts.

"They're past rehabilitation," stated Sissie. "Generations of venereal disease and every other loathsome ailment has made the whole race of them unfit for living."

Between Albion and myself we'd finished the evening's repast, and this orgy of inedible garbage was followed by the depths of depression. Let the women prattle; Albion and I knew—our luck had run dry.

But why?

What extravagant sin of mine had earned me this horrible end?

Numerous extravagant sins came to mind.

Would it were mine to do again, how simple a life I would lead.

"November three," said Albion in a strange singsong voice as of someone reading, "ship boarded and taken by enemy. November four, locked in the brig. Mood of crew, lower'n whale dung."

Our captain, I realized, was dictating to his log. We awaited the rest of the entry in respectful silence.

"During the last war," he informed us, "Nazi U-boats landed off Maine. Worst place they could of picked. Small-town folks is curious."

What, I wondered, does this unconnected kernel of maritime history have to do with our present predicament?

"The sea is everyone's friend," he said glumly, "and everyone's grave."

"Not mine," I retorted. (Isn't it odd how another person's gloom seems unreasonable? I'd just been thinking much the same thoughts, but now that Albion spoke with such philosophical certainty, I felt he was being unduly negative.)

The skipper's whiskered visage smiled dourly in the darkness. "'Tis," he replied succinctly.

"'Tis yourself," I countered. If there was one thing we didn't need for our spirits it was a pessimistic old New Englander, at their best, cheerful as lead pipes in the ground.

"Ayuh," said Albion, "we're goin' to a watery end."

This was too much. Very few would be bright and chipper at such moments, but Albion had surrendered hope utterly.

Or was the old salt playing possum?

There was a peculiar glint in his flinty eye, which looked like deranged activity, but might be brilliant scheming. Perhaps he was thinking, just as I, of being someplace else, and wondering how to get there.

"Fielding's very persuasive," said Julia in her strained cheerful voice.

Fielding . . . I realized again.

It's Fielding who holds my life in his hands.

Fielding is the thin gossamer thread between me and the sharks.

Have I acted so as to be worth saving? I wondered. Are the little art treasures I found for Fielding enough? Have my wit and patient ear given Fielding a positive, fatherly (almost) attitude toward me?

I reflected, and knew: They have not.

Fielding did not think of me as his son, or nephew, or of the slightest importance. My only link to Fielding was Julia. But she, I could see—". . . poor boys. So little opportunity for education, such little chance to develop appreciations. If only someone could take them in hand . . ."—was hopelessly confused.

Still, there was Sissie—". . . don't seem to realize we have *rights*. Guaranteed by international law . . ."

Which left only Albion. "These are troubled seas," the old carp muttered. "We're bein' stewed in this tent like Methodist Hell."

"Is it a tent?" inquired Julia with interest. "I thought it was a shack."

"We're hangin' by the gills," he intoned morosely. "They caught the starfish in their net."

"How sad," cried Julia, her compassion running thoroughly amok, directed at pirates, cutthroats, and now starfish.

"Can't be helped," insisted Albion, "that's the luck of the seas."

I turned on our captain. "I have had enough of your Down East wisdom for one evening. Would you please—as I believe the saying goes—stow it."

"Ayuh, she's stowed all right," replied the skipper. "Stowed deep."

Is he talking in code? I wondered. Or is he too going senile on us?

Either way, it didn't sound like a feasible plot for escape.

No, I mused, I have only mine own self to depend on.

Therefore, mine own self: Think.

But I could only think really creatively reclining on a Louis Seize daybed, or seated at a charming café table—certainly not hunkered down in the dark without so much as a copy of some cheering magazine of the arts. How could anyone be expected to scheme under such conditions? If I were fit for scheming at all, it was in the ambience of another century, court intrigue possibly, but not this squalid squatting under a roof of banana leaves.

I admitted the impossibility of saving my own skin.

And torpor set in.

Have you ever, I wonder, ridden on a Greyhound bus for four days? Perhaps when very young and poor and hoping to be discovered in Hollywood? Torpor sets in rather quickly on Greyhounds —it's either that or go crazy—and, gradually, it deepens.

I stretched my body out as well as I could, thinking, It's all up with this plaything of fate called Pluckrose, this mildly clever designer, sunken way past his depths, into the unadorned, un-trimmed, undecorated, unlit four walls of a barbarous hovel.

A ray of light suddenly entered; the moon had pierced

the cracks in the hut, and a second swarm of angry insects bombarded my frail flesh, their gourmand aggression plunging me more deeply into torpor.

Sinister thumping sounds came from the distance. Native drums, I thought dully as I lay in my chains and my torpor and imagined the jungle outside, with the tropical moon sailing across the empty sky.

The Greyhound bus rolled through Ohio . . . Indiana . . . Illinois . . . Missouri . . . unspeakably dreary Kansas . . . Colorado . . . deeper . . . Utah . . . deeper . . . Nevada . . . I fell into the ultimate torpor, deathlike slumber . . . and dreams of wandering through Tiffany's.

9

THE MOSQUITOES WERE SURFEITED, SUNLIGHT filtered through leaves, and it grew too hot for sleep. I opened my eyes, perceiving immediately that the morning's agenda would not include Tiffany's. There was the iron pole, there my foot, chained to same, there were my three comrades in dark travail gazing at the walls of the hut and each other.

"Oh dear," murmured Julia.

I thought that summed the situation nicely; it was not a bad dream one could awake from, but a great deal worse. The single saving grace was that the leafy walls of our abode let in daylight as well as heat; I'd feared to dwell in round-the-clock shadow.

Sounds of morning activity mixed with the songs of tropical birds; there were men's gruff voices, and explosives, and another sound—of movement from the mountains. Our boiled breakfast was shoved into the hut, and imbibed by self and Albion, while Julia explained to the invisible shape on the other side of the door that the Scarsdale Diet recommended grapefruit for breakfast.

"But melon will do," she added graciously.

Sissie showed all indications of fasting forever, or until her hunger strike had drummed up so much worldwide media concern that the local government, sanctioned in the UN, freed its political prisoners.

After breakfast (or what proved to be lunch), we were unchained and taken outside; hope and fear pumped through my veins.

Each of us had a personal escort, mine being the chiseled young man with my Piaget watch; had this watch formed a bond between us, a brotherly knot which would save me? By brotherly gunpoint he led me into the woods and, pointing to said watch and my trousers, let me know in dumb show I had exactly five minutes to perform my morning functions.

Then he led me back to the hut and rechained me. The others returned at about the same time, Albion stoic, Julia more startled than ever, and Sissie furious; the guard assigned to our idealistic darling was the most downtrodden worker imaginable, with aforementioned Parma-violet lobotomy scar and a possibly lobotomy-related problem controlling his spittle, which drooled and dribbled in silvery gobs from either corner of his foul mouth. Had she relieved herself in full slavering gaze of this oppressed Third World proletarian? I suspected she'd sooner perish of uremic poisoning.

The rest of the morning passed uneventfully; I stared at my navel, which I'd heard was good for the brain, and noticed that the lovely round setting for the jewel of my belly button had diminished. In spite of eating Sissie's share of the food, I was evidently fading away and would soon be no more than a line in an island song.

I felt myself steadily weakening, until by noon I was limp as seaweed; I knew, if I could look in a mirror, I'd see a pale shadow of my former rosy self.

"Gregory's to blame for this," muttered Sissie, sulking in chains.

I gazed up at her wearily. She addressed the others in preacherlike tones: "I have a plan."

"Do you want me to take dictation?" I asked.

"One of us has to be bait," she went on, "and Gregory's the obvious choice. He'll go to the door and make noise, complaining about conditions. Then while they're busy hammering Gregory senseless, I'll strangle one with my chain and Albion will grab his gun."

Aside from its being the most ridiculous strategy imaginable, I felt an excusable repugnance toward my role in the plan.

"'Twon't work," said our captain, and spat; he seemed to have an alternate scheme in his inscrutable mind, but didn't reveal it.

Sissie turned on me. "It's all your fault," she repeated.

"Why, pray tell?" I asked from the depths of my misery.

"Because you didn't leap at their throats while you had the chance. You had plenty of opportunity, I saw you."

"Sissie . . ." I said, lowering my head, but said no more; I'd had no opportunities except those connected with staring down the barrel of a submachine gun while a crazed and drooling cretin ordered me around with same.

"You should've jumped them," she insisted.

"Oh, go jump yourself," I snapped somewhat peevishly.

"Now children," said our gracious hostess, "don't quarrel. I'm sure everything will turn out fine."

As Julia spoke, the door pushed open, and I was overwhelmed by the aroma of coffee; no coffee was offered. Instead, Julia's one-toothed old guard entered, unbound her, and led her outside; as the door shut behind them, I thought I glimpsed Fielding's robust figure seated beside the hut, sipping from a large cup.

What could it mean?

Were they going to let Fielding and Julia free, and kill the rest of us?

And what of the coffee?

Strange to say, I fixated more on the coffee than freedom. I am one of those people whose day doesn't officially begin until they've imbibed three piping-hot cups of very strong, freshly ground, French-roast coffee, preferably accompanied by a single egg (when scrambling, a clove of garlic should be affixed to the tines of your fork, but not allowed to fall into the finished product) and thin buttered toast spread with bitter Seville marmalade. A swig of amoeba water, accompanied by boiled roots and berries (or whatever on earth they were giving us), even if prepared with the best will in the world, simply wasn't the same.

I hadn't, I realized, had a cup of coffee in days. My head

was throbbing with acute caffeine deprivation. Small wonder I couldn't think straight.

From the brief whiff I'd been treated to, it had smelled like excellent coffee. Even lousy coffee smells fairly good, but this brew, the more I dwelled on it, gradually loomed as having possessed the bouquet of award-winning beans, double roasted, finely ground, and perfectly extracted. For coffee of such caliber, one would trade one's new Piaget watch, if it hadn't already been traded.

Husband and wife conferred for an hour, and Julia was returned to our midst, wearing a look of bulldog determination not unlike Fielding's own bullish look.

Discreetly, we didn't gather round her for details, nor did she volunteer them, but after a bit, she motioned me to her side, and we held whispered tête-à-tête.

The shock to her nerves seemed to have somewhat abated. She spoke almost intelligibly, though her deep alto quivered.

"We must be prepared for self-sacrifice, Gregory."

I gazed at her in alarm.

"Each one of us," she added, "personally."

However, you see, it wasn't each one of us she was telling this to, but only me.

"In ordinary life," she said, "one lives according to codes, but some of us, at times, for the greater good, must live outside these false moral structures."

I heard Fielding in her words; it was practically his motto (not to mention Karl Marx's): The end justifies the means.

She went on in this vein, about the self-sacrifice I must be ready to make, and all the time I thought, Oh Lord, what does she want me to do?

I recalled my vow to help her, and seemed to hear distant music, my dying line in the calypso song: *He was just a sacrifice in de moonlight, de moonlight*

A lifetime of study gone down the drain. I pictured the marvelous houses I'd yet to decorate, the affairs of the heart ahead of me, the joys I would never know. I sagged, clinging to the leaves of the hut. I fell into my chain. My life membership in the Metropolitan Museum must go unused.

"So you understand and agree, I knew you would"—she stroked my hand—"dearest Gregory."

When darkness fell, we were fed our second slop of the day and again taken outside by our respective thugs.

He was a sacrifice in de moonlight, de moonlight percussed through my brain, and I dreaded the rise of that bright orb.

My guard, the connoisseur of fine watches, Miguel, returned me to the hut and my chain; stoic Albion was also returned; furious *Sissie* ditto; but not so Julia. She did not come back.

Albion, Sissie, and I lay in the dark being bitten by mosquitoes, and Albion wrote in his log: "November five, Mrs. Hale overboard."

It grew blacker, and the moon rose, shining ominously through the cracks in our hut. And still we waited for Julia's return.

"Feared lost at sea," muttered Albion.

From the remote interior came the savage cries I'd heard the previous night and the sound of slow hoofbeats winding down the mountains. A vicious and wild atmosphere prevailed.

And still there were just three of us.

"'Twas the seventh wave what called her aft."

I stared through a pillow-level crack in the wall at the grimly terrifying moon, from which I expected no mercy. I began to pray, to the sky and the stars, to save me. But this prayer, as had all my others, fell into emptiness.

I dozed. I awoke . . .

Julia was creeping back into our midst, accompanied by her one-toothed old guard, who refastened the chain round her ankle and scuffled out of the hut.

I waited until the door locked behind him, then moved to her side; the others were sleeping. I questioned her with my eyes.

She lowered her lids in reply.

"What happened?" I whispered.

Her lips started to tremble; I thought she might cry.

"Julia, you must tell me, are they going to kill us?"

"Worse."

I stifled a sob. Torture then. Mutilation and *Kaiserschmarren.*

"The worst thing there is," she said.

Worse than *Kaiserschmarren?* I gazed at her wildly.

"It's done," she whispered.

"It is?"

She pointed toward the closed door. "He . . . he . . ." He he?

In one tumultuous, blinding, hideous insight, the truth penetrated my obtuse skull.

That one-toothed fiend . . . and Julia. I clutched her hand. "Oh, my dear."

Her lips trembled again. She turned away. My pity couldn't have been more terrible if it had been my own wretched body, and not this poor brave grandmother's, sacrificed in de moonlight.

With infinite tenderness, I stroked her poor old brow until she finally twitched off to sleep.

In the moonlight a grimace tormented her face. Poor darling, I thought; then the grimace broadened into a faint smile, and then her entire face was wreathed in smiles. Her body stretched languidly. A soft snore of contentment rippled her limbs.

I gazed long at her voluptuous slumber.

Oh, you wicked old woman.

10

IN THE LEAST DESIRABLE HOVEL, MAN WILL STAKE
out his territory; mine was a stand of dirt adjacent to a certain
crack in the leafy wall. This slit became my obsession—eyes,
ears, and source of lavish conjecture. Through this slit in
the leaves, I maintained my identity, my illusion of freedom.

I discovered our camp to be a place of marketing activity.
The continual movement down from the mountains consisted
of mules laden with cargo and bound for the docks. The
men leading the packtrains were, for the most part, black
and incredibly strong; they carried almost as much as their
animals.

On our third morning I saw one of the drivers collapse
beneath the weight of his bale, while the rest of the procession
continued, filing robotlike past his crumpled body. They
eventually carried him off, but his poor crumpled form
remained with me, as a persistent ghostly presence, fate
unknown.

There was another type of individual also dwelling
in the hills— khaki-and-camouflage-clad Che Guevara
look-alikes—who occasionally wandered into our camp.
The meaning of the shots and explosives I'd been hearing
became all too clear; they were not dynamiting for the glory
of progress and septic systems; I was residing in the very
thick of mercenaries and guerrillas.

One could only shudder.

If ever an interior designer was outside his métier, this
took the pear-gingerbread-upside-down cake.

A third category visited our campsite, arriving in army vehicles from the direction of the docks—guests who entered the compound not at gunpoint, but as senators and advisers might enter the White House. And to me, chained in a hot stinking hovel, squinting through my green aperture, the main residence did begin to seem as glamorous as the Taj Mahal or Ten Downing Street.

This heavily guarded villa was a jungle jewel, lovely as any I'd seen in the Virgins. A house abandoned one year in the tropical bush has the look of an ancient ruin, overgrown by vegetation; therefore, the goal of the architect is to strike a picturesque medium between civilization and chaos, which our hosts had achieved by employing native woods, simplicity, and a touch of rococo about the carved gates, porch, and balconies. Elevated on stilts, adorned with graceful gables, and veiled by luxuriant foliage, it floated within my slim range of vision as the most alluring of creatures; I yearned to mount its piazza strung with lights in the evening; I envied the servants passing in and out of its portals; I caught glimpses of the interior and was filled with desire, inspired to change and rearrange a few pieces of furniture.

Idle fantasy, Gregory. You will yourself soon be furniture for some scuttling crab, who will take up residence in your pelvis— unless you slip your ball and chain.

Fielding remained in conference—thriving, I thought bitterly. Cigar smoke trailed from the porch, where he met his distinguished visitors; interviews wound on till dawn; stocks were signed away; corporations were juggled; Fielding continued to play.

Or so I imagined.

Inside the hut, Sissie fasted. I suppose it was her revolutionary background—Irish fanatics, macrobiotics, and so forth. Personally, I considered it the most tasteless display; as if things weren't bad enough, we'd soon have a bag of bones on our hands. Her accusations against me persisted: "You've let them walk all over us," she shouted.

"I'm tied to a stake," I screamed and, with a muffled sob, put my head between my knees.

"That's right," she continued, "hide from your responsibility."

Meanwhile, Albion, that enigma, was definitely thinking. I could see lugubrious thoughts march in procession beneath his duckbilled cap. It was possible he might still be our savior, despite a certain lack of scruples regarding the apportionment of food; the man was crafty and knew the elements.

"Up and down the mast," he reported to his log. "The young woman's all humped up like a hog goin' to war and the old woman's taken to canoodlin'."

Poor darling Julia. I thought of her as our own private Boule de Suif, the courageous Maupassant heroine who sacrifices her charms to a detested German officer to gain her fellow Frenchmen their freedom.

And as darkness fell that evening, our heroine grew strangely restive.

Footsteps were heard outside, followed by a low hoarse chuckle; Julia's ears appeared to perk up. She touched her hands to her hair. The bamboo door was unlocked. A single tooth gleamed in the moonlight.

Her guard lumbered in, unchained her, and led her away to defile her.

"Puts me in mind," remarked Albion, "of a lady in Bath who took to grassin' nights with a plumber's assistant."

Taking the more classic Maupassant view, I retorted, "It's hardly the same."

"She's full of weasel juice."

The following morning Julia was in possession of several items from the *Hale Fellow II*—her silk cosmetic case, magnifying mirror, reading matter, vitamin pills, and the little portable writing desk we'd bought in L-port.

I examined this odd choice of treasures, puttering especially mournfully around the pretty little lap desk.

"Please take it," said Julia (always so generous), "and any one of the books."

You may ask, what did I need with a mother-of-pearl-inlaid Victorian lap desk? Shouldn't it, rather, have gone to our captain, who was keeping the log? But it would be such a comfort, I felt, to draw up my last will and testament on a gracious writing board.

For reading matter, I chose Father Labat's *Nouveau Voyage aux Isles de l'Amérique*.

Scarcely had I plunged into the divine preface when our door was flung open, and in reeled one of the khaki-clad soldiers from the hills, eyes bloodshot, ear bandaged, beret askew; with a drunken gaze round the company and a happy-go-lucky grin, he lunged for our fair Sissie.

That practiced maiden drew back her leg and gave her new admirer the very same kick that had driven the exiled prince to his royal knees on the beach; this time, however, her girlish spirit held many days of smoldering rage. The drunk soldier buckled in two, his face a dim chartreuse, and backed out of the hut in a manner suggesting severe internal complications.

No one said a word until our captain made log summation: "She put the oakum to him."

"At least," said Sissie, "I stood up for my rights."

"We applaud what you've done," I agreed, hoping revenge would not fall on us at once.

"I did what you should've done."

"I don't kick people in the groin, if I can possibly avoid it."

"No, of course not. Life for you is just one big Victorian fainting sofa."

"If only we had one," I sighed: hand-carved mahogany with biscuit-tufted brocade in a pattern of geraniums.

"You've betrayed us to the end," she declared.

"Aren't you slightly fixated on my supposed guilt? Perhaps you have other reasons for disliking me."

"I could think of many."

"The feeling is mutual."

"Now children," said Julia, "we've all been under a strain, but I think we're coming out of it now." Julia was coming out of her blouse, which she'd recently taken to wearing in a most décolleté fashion.

Sissie puffed up like a pigeon. "I won't allow them to touch me."

"That's right," I agreed, "no one has ever touched you. You should be given an award for purity."

Fire flashed in her eyes. (How low I'd fallen, that my only pastime was mocking poor Sissie's celibacy.)

Returning to the *Nouveau Voyage aux Isles de l'Amérique,* I read a description of local cuisine which did little to set me at ease; if native Carib tastes nowadays were anything like in the good father's time, we'd soon be flambéed *en brochette* with salt, crushed pimento, and lime juice, and dished up for dinner on *balisier* leaves.

At evening the now-familiar, low, chortling sound outside our hut was repeated. We glanced toward Julia, who was hurriedly primping in her magnifying mirror.

Coarse voice from without.

Door unlocked . . .

An eighteen-karat watch glinted in the dark.

It wasn't Julia's guard, but mine, the young and chiseled Miguel.

Had he come for *me?*

Or for high-kicking Sissie?

No, it was Julia's chain he unlocked.

She looked surprised, then flustered, then—it pains me to report —the old strumpet flushed with delight.

"Happy as a clam at high tide," noted Albion on the heels of her exit. "The plumber's assistant, as I recollect, was just about the same age as that feller."

I lay awake, pondering, for several hours, until our heroine returned, tiptoeing in a manner both languid and confident as well as somewhat giddy. She fell asleep immediately, heaving great sighs of love. Her metamorphosis struck me a heavy blow. Why had the young Miguel taken a woman of seventy for a stroll beneath tropical stars? Apparently, Julia's delightful vivacity translated well into the sack, and word had gone out.

How easily, I saw, reality shifts.

Plunging into philosophy for solace, I slowly began to perceive what makes the world tick. It is an underlying something that is tapped according to circumstance. Julia had tapped it and had found the fountain of youth. By the pale moonlight flickering in through the leaves, I watched her roll and heave and smile the deep satisfaction of rebirth.

Morning revealed her fresh and chipper; she glowed.

At this point it became hard to ignore the odd fact that though she didn't partake of our filthy meals, she was growing, if anything, *embonpoint* I, for one, assumed this becoming plumpness was not due to the calories in smugglers' semen but, rather, that our Boule de Suif was being fed elsewhere.

"Please, Gregory, you eat my portion," she murmured with a smile of noblesse oblige; low company hadn't made her one whit less the lady.

I don't know if I've ever mentioned that Julia had pretty good legs. Now she saw no point in concealing her light under a bushel, nor under slacks for that matter.

Her garments grew, quite frankly, tattered before their time. Surely six days in a hut wouldn't contrive to fray one's trousers raggedly off mid-thigh; nor would the normal wear and tear of scarcely a week rend such well-placed rips and pluck away two very strategic blouse buttons. Because of this sad loss of buttons, Julia was soon forced to tie her blouse up at the waist, revealing a tan strip of midriff. And then she found (or was given) a gay-colored kerchief to bind her hair; proceeded to lose one gold earring; and the effect was complete: Mrs. Fielding F. Hale—a pirate's wench.

But wasn't that, in a way, what she'd been most of her life?

Oh, how I longed for the touch of home, for a museum café, for an issue of *Gourmet*.

And Sissie continued her torment.

"Look at you," she hissed, "sitting and moping, while Julia's being violated daily."

I glanced up, startled at this. "Violated?"

"How dare you suggest anything else? In any event, you were supposed to protect her."

"I was supposed to pick out her furniture."

"You have no sense of loyalty, of honesty. If only I were a man, I'd show them."

"Show them what, your tennis racquet? Don't be a fool, these people are murderers."

"You make me sick."

"I'll try to keep out of your world," I said huffily, adjusting my chain.

"You have no fiber. You never did."

"I have lots of fiber. I'm living on straw like a goat, I'm filled with bamboo leaves, I'm . . ." The rest of my retort was lost in babble. Life wasn't painful enough, I had to have Sissie too.

The horrible girl wasn't eating, rarely drinking, for all I knew, never evacuating. From having been antiseptically clean, she now fairly rattled with bits of caked mud on the cuffs of her jeans; her strawberry hair hung greasy and limp; what she needed was a gay-colored kerchief, for starters, and certainly some wholesome boiled twigs.

"You must eat," I admonished her.

"Why?"

Why indeed should I care? My sense of loyalty, of honesty. "This is no time," I said, "for self-destructive heroics. If we somehow manage to escape and have to run through the jungle, you'll need every ounce of slop you can get."

"Do you think," she asked contemptuously, "that *you 're* going to lead us out of this?"

"How do you know what I'm capable of?" I snapped, knowing myself incapable of any exertion more demanding than raising a cracker of caviar to my lips. I glared at her defiantly, as if I happened to have a plan of escape all worked out.

"I repeat," she tapped an arrogant foot, "why should I eat?" Her formerly pugged face was haggard and gaunt; her freckles swelled with the bites of tropical bugs; the famous Hale bosom had wilted.

"For humanity," I said. "You must stay alive not for yourself, but so you can save the world, contribute your wisdom and skills to the nations of man." I went on in this flattering vein, comparing her to other great women of history—Joan of Arc, Madame Defarge, Bertha Krupp, and Nancy Reagan.

That evening she forced herself to swallow two handfuls of our disgusting repast, and Albion, I'm pleased to say, didn't appear to begrudge a starving woman two mouthfuls. "Just the very same as Ethelred's cow," he noted, possibly for the ship's log.

Then came the Hour of Sacrifice.

Heavy footfalls outside the hut. Guttural laughter. Julia straightens one gold earring. Bamboo door pushes open.

And there stood the lobotomy case, dribbling from both corners of his revolting mouth, Parma-violet scar scarlet in anticipation.

If the face of the guest was unexpected, Julia cloaked her dismay as every well-seasoned hostess must.

The gentleman approached her chain in a stooping sideways shuffle, reminiscent of the Hunchback of Notre Dame, and our charmer sailed across the mud floor of the hut, hand extended, as if welcoming the Argentinian ambassador to her ballroom.

What élan, I thought. What star quality.

I could not, in all honesty, feel that freedom for us was in any possible way connected with Julia selling her body to this Cro-Magnon gentleman who sported every appearance of having just gnawed on the uncooked leg of an animal he'd strangled barehanded. On the contrary, I felt the transaction to be a very temporal and personal thing on the part of this lowest man on the decision-making totem pole, resulting no doubt in a pleasant few hours for him, but certainly not escape for dear Julia, no matter how graciously she surrendered her chastity.

Fluttering, glittering, she glided out on his filthy arm.

Our captain made log entry: "Yessir, that lady in Bath had a heat pump installed in her house as a tribute."

Sissie glanced at us both in disgust and lay down on her spot in the mud.

I took my post beside the wall's peephole:

Julia and her dribbling abductor were wending their way toward the docks, or more likely to some trysting place in the same direction but not so far down.

The drums started.

The veranda lanterns were lit at the villa.

Far away in Manhattan, friends without a care in the world, other than how best to enjoy the evening, were sitting down to dine at Lutèce.

In a charming brownstone on Madison Avenue, my lovely next-door neighbor was putting our song on the record player.

Chained to a pole at the end of the world, belching monkey stew, un-wined, unwashed, unwanted except by mosquitoes, I stood sweating at a slit of green leaves, and wondered, What atrocity will tomorrow bring?

The sun set in a blood-red sky.

11

"It isn't really," Julia confessed to me, "technically, rape. They can't help themselves," she sighed. "They're so high-spirited."

I readily agreed; they were capital fellows, and for all I cared, she could sell her faded charms every hour, because the transaction had richly paid off: We were confined, but no longer chained.

It's plain from my attitude, I'm the type who would sell his own mother if the going got rough. *The situation is delicate,* I wrote in my mental diary. *Julia has taken to sleeping with pirates.*

The mental effort of note-taking beyond me, I gave up after two lines. But the situation did remain delicate; I was sleeping with centipedes. Our end was in sight, but at least dear Julia was enjoying herself; she might've been entertaining on Nantucket.

Albion nodded sagely. "I seen queer things before," he muttered. "Seen ladies behind the chip pile with rumdums and sawdust sorters." He gazed through his crack in the palm leaves. Outside, the endless caravan of natives and pack animals wound their way down from the mountains. "That's the gang you'll be workin' with," he predicted. "Work till you drop."

"Here now," I said, "don't suggest such a thing."

"Seen a donkey bite a man once, pretty near took the hide off of him."

"Is that so?" I asked calmly.

"Yep, I heard them talkin' about you. I speaks a little Spanish. They cal'ate you'd make an able muler. You'll carry the mule when he gets tired."

"Albion, how can you joke at a time like this?"

"Dunno." The dour skipper removed his beaked cap and rubbed his grizzled head. "Just the way I'm built, I guess."

He resumed staring out through his palm leaves.

Behind us the door was unlocked; the fragrance of freshly brewed coffee heralded a visit from Fielding. Julia was let out for the meeting, and before the door slammed shut, I caught a glimpse of my former employer.

Fielding was not at his best. If Julia, since her sacrifice, could pass for a woman of sixty, her husband had the air of a man of ninety.

"We've been unfavorably impacted," he said dully.

I pressed my ear to the wall.

"We've lost everything," he told her. "Except a few factories in Hong Kong."

"Poor darling," she murmured with sympathy, but also a distinct air of distraction.

"They've bankrupted me. They've crushed me. They've broken my back. They're bleeding me dry." His words caught in his throat. "They're holding me in their grip and squeezing."

This struck me keenly. I feared they would squeeze Fielding and throw him away, then squeeze me in turn, from which would emerge only a few drops of something, and that would be my last bit of earthly business—planting a lone Alpine edelweiss in the tropics.

"They've got an aggressive infrastructure, a sharp team of lawyers, their own banks . . ." I thought I caught the name of a financial institution; Fielding lowered his voice. "But Fielding F. Hale's not quite the fool he may seem. Reactive planning and procedural safeguards . . ." He now spoke too softly for me to hear.

The situation is beyond him, I thought.

Or is nothing beyond the rich man?

I felt my own insignificance; I was merely a flea on

Fielding's tail. The flea bath would come, and I'd be washed down the drain, into the local sewage system, the sea.

Albion is right: We are shark food. We are lost. How ghastly, I thought, glancing at Sissie, who sat in the mud, simmering in her own juices, her foolish pug face furrowed with futile fantasies of revenge; the girl was an idiot, but I felt for her and wished to help her escape.

This heroic urge dimmed, and faded. Some are cut out for heroism, and others only for daydreaming. (For an instant I seemed to feel a helping hand on my brow, but knew it was just vain illusion. We were prisoners and *they* numbered hundreds; how could anyone make his way through such a gang? Hopeless, I thought, it's hopeless.)

Sissie glanced my way and, automatically, the same scratchy old record started to play:

"Gregory, what's happened to Julia is disgusting. We've got to risk our lives and save her from these nightly abductions."

"I rather suspect she wouldn't appreciate our help."

"You mean she prefers to absorb all our punishment herself?"

"I mean she's having the time of her life. Haven't you heard her sighs in the moonlight?"

"Pig!"

"Possibly. But I've been around some, dear, and know what sighs are."

"If they try to touch *me* ..."

"You'll kick them in the balls; yes, Sissie, we're well acquainted with your mating dance."

"What a vile man you are."

"I suppose."

"I hate a coward."

"I'd love it if you would shut up."

"I want us to fight them."

"And I am not moving from this stake."

"You have no guts, you have no . . ."

"Pluck," I supplied. How could I tell this raving creature that it takes me simply ages to get going?

(But faintly, within, I felt the stirring of the ancient clan of Pluckroses slowly rising up from their couch.)

The next voice that penetrated my gap in the wall was Julia's, sounding troubled. "We'll be sent home?"

"My feasibility studies," replied Fielding, "indicate an optimized interface, a viable scenario for the procurement of freedom for you, me, and Sissie."

"But I can't leave the boys . . . that is, Gregory and Albion."

Fielding ignored this statement and spoke of cutting his losses.

Julia returned to the hut with a preoccupied air.

"Don't worry," I said to her bitterly, "you'll be okay." I, of course, would be edelweiss.

She sighed and shook her head. "Nobody appreciates him."

I'd never really thought of my employer as an undervalued being, and gazed at Julia questioningly. She was wearing her faraway look—that radiant expression which had come to her recently and certainly had nothing to do with Fielding.

"Shockingly unappreciated," I agreed, dying to know of whom we were speaking.

She ran a finger dreamily along the breadth of her forehead. "Did he ever tell you," she asked in tender tones, "how he acquired his scar?"

Only one gentleman of my acquaintance possessed such a scar— the slobbering moronic brute who shoved me in the solar plexus half a dozen times daily and took out our Julia every fourth night.

"I never suspected a man could be so sensitive," she murmured, "so gentle . . ."

I begged to differ, and tried, in the most tactful way, to point out that I was being starved and beaten regularly by the same criminal whom she was praising.

My words went unheeded; she was beyond reach and reason. With a spasm of despair I realized she'd been bewitched, besotted, and besmitten by the most hideous of her tryst fellows. Growing more vibrant, she confided that the fiend possessed the most remarkable *je ne sais quoi* she'd ever seen in a man, considering his lack of advantages.

"What would he be," she asked, "if he had Fielding's education?"

I didn't honestly believe the man was educable, but when has it ever availed to argue with a woman in love?

That night I lay with my face in the dirt, wallowing in abject misery, knowing my time was fast waning. I wished the whole thing were over and I but a sprig of dainty edelweiss, and yet I was too cowardly to wish it from the heart. I tried again to pray, but what was the use? What was out there to hear me? What god? What angel? What spirit of nature?

A digging, snooting sound came from the ground outside, approximately three feet from my head.

12

FIELDING LIMPED INTO OUR SHELTER AT NOON, looking like felled Yorkshire pudding, and gathered us around him.

"They're not going to free us."

"But I thought . . ." interrupted Julia.

"Inoperative," he answered in lifeless tones. "I'm beaten. And not just on paper."

". . . Then we aren't leaving?"

"Ain't leavin'," repeated Albion, doubtless for the ship's log.

Fielding lifted a shaking hand to his pocket and unearthed a Montecristo No. 1 pure Havana. "I've managed to save our skins. For whatever that's worth."

"All five skins?" I hastily inquired.

He nodded, his own skin the color of Gorgonzola, and proceeded to speak, half to us, half to himself, while his guard sat outside in the sunshine idly picking his teeth with a bayonet.

"I'll run it through for you briefly. *El jefe's* been targeting for a foothold in the Far East for years. And I've got the factories in Hong Kong, with all the contacts and leverage needed to facilitate the front he's been seeking. Which is why he let me hold on to those particular factories." Fielding plunged his cigar into the air. "It's a very lackluster feeling, I can tell you, to be a pawn in somebody else's empire, a saddle for somebody else's free ride." He caught hold of his emotions, sucked his cigar. "For whatever time frame I'm useful, I'll be permitted to live. I'll be taken out, occasionally, and paraded—in Hong Kong or wherever—to show I'm alive. There'll be the usual information dissemination process; it'll be rumored I've found my West Indian Tahiti, where I happily dwell with my wife, my niece, my ship captain, and my decorator." He gazed at us each in turn. "Other wealthy men have turned recluse, gone windy in their old age." He puffed vigorously on his cigar, and its familiar aroma belied the stinking green hut, the guard outside, the strange words he was speaking. "That's the official scenario. The truth is, we'll live like dogs. Like hoi polloi." His voice all but broke. "Like my own factory workers."

"Back to the tiller," remarked Albion.

"Yes, you'll be employed on the boats."

"And you and I?" asked Julia. "Will we have to work too?"

He gazed at his wife in her one gold earring, pirate scarf, and gay dishabille. "I'm sure, my dear, you will make yourself indispensable, as always."

"What about me?" Sissie demanded.

He looked at her with distaste. "Unfortunately, you're a young woman without any marketable skills whatever. Therefore, you'll have to learn, shall we say . . . flexibility." His dull eyes lingered on his niece, and I could perceive, hovering beneath his enormous regrets, his overwhelming regrets, his tragic regrets, was the same irritation dear Sissie always inspired in those around her.

He turned to me. "I'm sorry, Gregory. We've all got to do things we might not choose. I wasn't able to sell you as an interior designer." He hesitated, and reached into his pocket as if to offer me a cigar, then realized it was needless to go quite that far. "You'll work with the mules."

A face flashed before me, the face of the driver who'd collapsed under his bale; and then the bale itself flashed before me; never, in my most *outré* Mr. Universe fantasies, could I possibly lift such a weight off the ground; it was all I could manage to lift the corner of a crooked picture on the wall. "Mules?" I said quickly. "Feeding them? Grooming them?"

"Don't be an ass, Pluckrose. Mules aren't groomed. You'll work with the pack trains. I'm sorry, but that's what they've decided."

"Did you tell them about Gregory's cucumber soup?" interjected Julia. "Everyone enjoys that sort of soup in hot weather."

"We're all coming down in the world," he said curtly. "There's a redundancy here of human resources, and diversification is in order. I've done what I could."

"When do I start?" I asked weakly; it wasn't a memorable condemned man's last line, but seemed painfully relevant.

"In a couple of days."

It's amazing what charm a fetid, green steambath of a bug-ridden hut can hold, when set against the prospect of hernia, death, and trampling by mules. I would've happily stayed in our little hovel forever, eating fricasseed lizard and being shoved in the solar plexus half a dozen times daily; at least it was on the plane of existence I'd grown so accustomed to—earthly life.

It was a dreadful afternoon.

Everyone sat around sunk in self-pity, except for Julia, who tried her best to look sorrowful, without succeeding.

I clearly required a miracle. I needed one of those pirate chiefs—*el jefe*—to see what an effective decorator could do with a dirt-floored prison: the touch of some heavy oak chairs, perhaps, circa Spanish Inquisition, trimmed in brass and angled to catch the light.

Either that, or a natural calamity. I recalled the conversation we'd had on the yacht about the murderer Ludger Sylbaris, who'd survived the turn-of-the-century eruption of Mount Pelée in his thickly walled underground prison, alone of thirty thousand people. Why couldn't a local volcano kill every smuggler on the island, except for me and my party, with the possible exception of Sissie? After which I'd charter us a plane back to Maine, where we would promptly build a fire in the fireplace and sip some nice hot chocolate.

But no, this is my reality, pacing circles round a stake in

the ground, weak, weary, and soon to be carrying a donkey on my back.

Where are my *Architectural Digests?* Where is Soho? Where are my frequent visits to great museums?

The truth, the bitter truth, is that I shall see none of this again. I am without an ally. (I thought Albion might do, but he has such a perverted sense of humor. And Julia is carrying on so.) I have no one. I have been abandoned by the human race. The light of morning does not find me eagerly springing toward some new decorating project. I have rearranged my chain in all its possible combinations with stake and shadow of bamboo, and now I don't even have a chain.

I have no creative resources left.

I am alone.

To distract my tortured mind I read Père Labat's description of Caribbean diseases and realized I'd come down with leprosy.

All the symptoms were there—numbness in the extremities, pale blotches, curling of fingers, and a sickly sweet smell. (Though the smell, I admitted, might've come from eating sautéed tarantula.)

After a sickening supper of same, Julia disappeared with the Parma-scarred gentleman. Through my crack in the wall, I watched them walk along the path to their tryst; one could see by the quantity of his dribbles it was the real thing for both of them.

Albion tossed in his sleep, muttering, "Tail the mains'l sheet . . . There's a capful o' wind . . . Fang the pumps . . ." and "Call for the butter."

Sissie, grinding her teeth, took a bit longer to slumber.

And, presently, I heard the sound I awaited.

The previous night's digging and snooting had brought the creature to just under my pillow; my intention now was to boldly dig down and meet it.

I'd been working my nerves to this point all day. I realized it might be anything—deadly, poisonous, venomous, vicious in fang and claw, grubular, hirsute, slimy, disgusting of feature, and foul of breath. But, on the other hand, why condemn a beast before you've seen it, a book before you've read it, or a souffle before you've eaten it? (Julia's lobotomized friend was a very good case in point.)

Having done so much work in advance, it didn't take the creature long to burrow and snuffle to its previous juncture, where I was stealthily scratching away at my end of the dirt.

Hearing a competitive digging above it, the beast paused in its own operation. I too paused, not to seem overly pushy, then resumed my scratching.

The moon was low, pouring its silvery sheen through the leafy cracks in the hut's eastern wall. The creature gave a frightened sneeze and seemed to retreat back into its burrow.

This emboldened me to dig faster; I tossed the dirt up in a heap and kept digging until I felt the earth grow thin.

A low squeaking note of undeniable terror rose from the crumbling ground.

"*Shhhh,*" I whispered.

The creature fell silent.

I pushed my fingers through the thin ground and was greeted by a black hole, then a second squeak, which turned into a sneeze.

Leaning on my stomach and elbows, I plunged my hand into the tunnel, met something cold and wet and tubular, and yanked back my hand. *Quelle horreur.* I had opened my home to a snake.

But what sort of snake snuffles and sneezes?

I put my face as close as I could to the hole without blocking the reflection of the moon altogether.

The tip of the snake slowly appeared under my porthole; I retreated, and the rest of the animal gradually proceeded, its serpentine tip proving to be a proboscis. Several inches behind this grotesque appendage, or several seconds in arrears, appeared two decidedly curious eyes.

We stared at each other's faces, or what we could see of each other's faces, neither, I fear, overwhelmingly impressed.

The eyes blinked; the appendage rose; and the beast's head was lifted, snout foremost, practically into my own.

It wasn't a large face nor, by any standards, attractive, but I felt it looked intelligent.

How does one know such things? For example, I knew instantly, when setting eyes on Julia's pal with the *violette de Parme* scar, that here was not a profound thinker. Some people are more difficult to judge—Albion, for instance. However, I instinctively felt this rubber-nosed creature had *it*.

Quietly, I sat back, to give the animal leeway should it wish to proceed further.

With a rather ungainly shifting of what I assumed were its hindquarters, it maneuvered itself until it had thrust its forepaws out of the hole.

I slowly offered my own right forepaw, which the creature gazed at for a moment. Then with a slushing, heaving, churning sort of motion, the animal popped completely out of its burrow.

There it hunched, in my hut, peering at me.

And there sat I, peering at it.

Behind us Sissie and Albion breathed deeply.

What does one say to a strange guest in the night?

Speech wasn't necessary.

The beast looked at me, and I looked at the beast, and I frankly wondered what the devil it could be.

Tropical fauna was not my strong suit.

It looked to me like a cross between a coatamundi and a tapir . . . it wasn't a raccoon or a pig, but a sort of pigcoon, whose habits included burrowing at night, under huts, and whose snout, in a pinch, could double for a flexible garden hose.

I offered my hand again.

But footsteps sounded outside the door; without a backward glance my new friend dove headfirst down its hole.

13

My guard Miguel, who wasn't a bad sort at all, took me by gunpoint next morning to see something very *lindo*.

Of course, we each have our own idea of beauty, but having already agreed on watches and, to a lesser extent, Julia, I was prepared for a pleasing sight—a nest of four blue eggs, perhaps, or a single perfect orchid.

He led me through the bush to a jutting rock, a barren spot cleared in the thicket, and pointed through a cleft in the trees: Far below, the harbor glittered. There was the narrow crocodile mouthful of sea where we'd landed, there the dock where we'd disembarked, and there a single perfect yellow battleship.

"Isn't she a beauty?" he asked.

As far as I knew, there was only one daffodil-colored destroyer in the world. My mind raced; had they captured the sheik who'd entertained us so regally that afternoon, lifetimes ago, in the Virgins?

"Friend of *el jefe*," said Miguel.

"Are you sure?" I asked stupidly.

"*Sí, sí*," Miguel nodded his head vigorously. "They are like two brothers together."

If the sheik and *el jefe* were even remotely like brothers together, I reasoned, this was hardly the local, illiterate, downtrodden den of Third World thieves I'd believed, but a multinational network of power so vast and far-reaching, I found myself going weak in the peritoneum.

Satisfied that I was properly impressed, Miguel importantly consulted his Piaget watch and escorted me back to my hovel, where Sissie and I held our final conversation.

She was staring out through a crack in the banana leaves; she turned to me. "We have one last chance," she said tensely. "When they grab me, you jump them."

I gazed at the poor fool in her dream. "Yes, of course, Sissie dear."

"Jump for the grub," our captain remarked to himself.

Sissie's face was twitching. "Then topple them and take their machine guns."

"All right, Sissie, I'll do that."

"Then blow them away, the vile things."

"Certainly, certainly."

"And if you're killed doing it, you can have the satisfaction of knowing you died a brave man."

"Yes, that will be comforting."

"So, are you ready?" she whispered.

"Yes, dear, I am, completely."

"Here they come."

I heard the approach of marching feet and metal clanking against metal, then presently found myself facing a bullet-headed individual with neck the size of a Sequoia redwood, in medal-festooned uniform and high shiny boots, carrying a long riding whip, and clicking his heels in a manner which made one think he might be a favorite son of one of the gentlemen of the previous era who found it so convenient to settle in Argentina around the time of the Nuremberg trials.

"Which of you," he asked, "kicked Comandante Guerrillero Alfredo Garcia in the testicles and put one of my best officers in the infirmary?"

Albion, Julia, and I gazed every way but toward Sissie. True, she was a trying companion, but we didn't wish to see her horsewhipped,

"Me," she snapped in her arrogant fashion.

Colonel Goose-step looked her over carefully, then inquired, "Do you like to join us?"

Without a moment's hesitation she barked, "Yes."

You could have knocked me over with a Parmesan biscuit.

"I heard," said the gentleman smiling—if you could call it a smile—"there was one *hombre* in this pack of dogs."

The beastly girl didn't deign to say good-bye to her former pack mates, but swaggered out, hair straggling, cuffs rattling with dirt, a real killer, born to the cause.

I wondered what cause it was, exactly.

"She found her hole in the beach," remarked our captain to his log. "But it's a foul bight, if you ask me."

I must say, it was much nicer without Sissie and her coarse nagging voice, though the situation wasn't heavenly under any circumstances. I gazed out through my crack in the leaves.

"Mules," said Albion, "are moody beasts."

"You seem to know something about them."

"Can't say as I'd wanna sail within hailin' distance." He spat through his crack in the wall. "Course, there is some fellers get along with a mule. 'Tis quite the sight too."

I received this information in silence.

"Mules," the captain mused, "been knowed to stave a lightweight man all to flinders."

"Oh, come now."

"Trample or disenable. A mule can be rugged." I continued watching the pack caravan winding down from the hills.

"Thar she blows," cried Albion. "Did you see the beast haul round and bite that feller between the face and the eyes?"

"My crack must be differently angled."

"That's alst we got," sighed the old man, "just a dim slit in a ding-busted bunch of banana leaves. I fear it makes a lad dull."

"Not you, Albion," I said comfortingly. "You're never dull."

"Dull as a knife," he replied, a glint in his eye.

Code? I wondered.

I sidled over to him. "Albion," I said softly, "we've got to escape."

"Not likely. Them boys has guns, and you and I got nought but bent spoons."

"There must be a way," I insisted. Dare I tell him of the tunneling in the night?

"There ain't no way but down, for the likes of you and me," he said, tugging at his cap beak, just before his guard appeared to take him off on his maiden cruise, transporting mind-enslaving drugs to innocent American youth, old people, and middle-aged congressmen.

"Bungs up and bilge free," were my captain's last words to me.

Exit Albion.

Which left only Julia.

She and I shared a good cry and she promised to use her influence with the guards, but when I made specific suggestions—that on her nightly outing she steal a pistol, dagger, or hand grenade— she smiled and answered, "Yes, dear," much as I had to Sissie, with no clear response in her dreamy blue eyes. She wished to use her influence with the guards mainly to educate them, clothe them, and possibly take them to the masked ball.

No, Julia was little help; which left only one companion in the dark, and he not even human, merely an animal. How could aid come from there? (A Pluckrose is always open to new ideas.)

To punctuate what little hope there was for my short-term survival, the guards brought no spider stew for my dinner. (Not that a Pluckrose can survive on such fare.) Dinner hour came and went, and Julia was led away to her permanent quarters.

"The mule team she will pick you up in the morning," said Miguel as he locked the hut door.

For the first time since our capture, I was alone.

The moon was just about rising.

Instantly, I flung away the soft dirt with which I'd disguised my hole of the previous evening and fell to the most furious digging.

I cursed the animal for being so small; if he'd been my size, I could've fled immediately through his burrow. As it was, I had only till morning to make the tunnel large enough for my own lissome form and to snatch my escape.

A sound came from the other end of the burrow—a familiar snooting, which gradually approached, until my hand encountered a wet rubbery nose.

"Out of my way," I ordered. "I don't have time to waste."

But the animal pushed against my hand with its snout and forced itself forward, making further work impossible. Then with its slushing, heaving, churning maneuver, it popped once more into my hut and stood, in all its homeliness, blinking good evening.

"Very well," I said, "good evening. But I can't spend time in small talk."

Having paused for civilities, I returned to my tunnel-widening activities.

The animal peered over my shoulder, snuffling with keen curiosity.

"You're blocking my moonlight," I said rather sternly.

It replied with a vigorous nudge of its chubby body and, edging me slightly to the right, fell to work digging beside me.

I believe that in animals with a strong burrowing instinct, the sight of burrowing of any kind sets them off like Pavlov's dogs. Its paws flailed, the dirt flew away, and our tunnel increased.

From a distance, I heard other activity—the crew of the battleship going back and forth in their launches. From the hills came the sound of explosives. The hellish drums struck up. What awaited one out there wasn't exactly one's cup of Darjeeling, but clearly it beat hernia, death, and mules.

We worked steadily, side by side; the beast's stamina was amazing for such a plump little creature; its snooting began to sound like words of encouragement. As we got deeper, I started to feel quite like Jean Gabin, digging his nocturnal tunnel to freedom alongside the little Jew with the mustache.

Grand illusion indeed. How ironic that an après-ski person such as myself should be thrown into a classic Renoir conflict.

Shoulder to shoulder we dug.

It was devilishly hot and I sweated like a pig, but my pig (or whatever in the world the rubber-nosed creature was) smelled like a clean, if asthmatic, puppy. Its warm snuffling breath being close to my neck, I was surprised how almost pleasant the foggy fragrance; could it be that the unseemly-looking beast subsisted on a diet more delicate than my own?

I reminded myself that my recent diet had been far from refined, my living conditions strikingly like the near-extinct mountain gorilla's, and doubtless my standards had taken a nosedive— which didn't make it less agreeable having such an inoffensive and conscientious companion burrowing like mad beside me, its warm dry fur grazing my skin in the most friendly manner imaginable, its snooting remarks neither wearisome nor demanding, and the entire effort, as far as reward went, strictly *pour moi*. When I saw how slow was the job and how grueling, I realized that without my assistant I wouldn't have stood a chance; even now, it wasn't a sure bet; the tunnel was long and time running short.

"Why," I asked the animal, "did you place your exit so far away?"

The eccentric engineer replied with an untroubled snort, which I assumed meant *I had my reasons,* and continued its indomitable digging.

We were deep in the burrow. Pitch dark. I worked solely by feel and my colleague's lead. I've always loathed confined spaces, and was reminded of a certain torture, so common on the silver screen of my childhood, where the walls are made to close in upon our hero until, in one more second, he'll be pressed Long Island duckling—*To Be Continued Next Week.*

Thank goodness for the animal's calm; I believe it kept me from going stark mad, from tearing blindly in every direction until my nostrils and eyes filled with dirt, and giving in to that fatal hysteria haunting every prisoner in every dark pit the world over, and every highly strung interior designer all the time.

The beast clearly knew his business. The situation we

were in was the merest ratatouille to him. Slimy worms and creepy insects falling helter-skelter around us didn't disturb his snuffling aplomb nor raise his diastole; on the contrary, he seemed to feel this was the gayest game imaginable, to be buried alive in the tropics on a Saturday night.

The sounds of the island had faded—the motor launches, drums, and explosives; we were lost in the bowels of the earth, digging blindly; or perhaps the creature could see? Yes, that must be the answer, I thought; that's why he's so nonchalant. I recalled a lecture series I'd once attended at the Museum of Natural History on optical rods (one *does* do these inexplicable things), and no sooner had I remembered the lecturer's rather poetic comparison between the eyes of a frog and Spinoza, then I too could see.

A Spinozistic miracle.

Or, light at the end of the tunnel.

A squeak came from my furry companion.

A silver beam of moonlight touched the distant tip of its snout.

I am free, I realized.

Leaving the competent beast to widen the last short stretch on its own, I shifted into reverse and crawled hurriedly backward through the burrow in the direction of the hut.

It was some problem rising feet foremost up into the chamber, and one might suggest I was performing a reckless and foolhardy deed, returning to possible capture when on the bright brink of freedom, but it was just the sort of act you might expect from Jean Gabin.

Without ceremony I slipped the volume containing Père Labat's essential descriptions of second- and third-stage leprosy into my little lap desk and plunged back into the burrow. It wasn't easy, creeping blindly through a constricted mud tunnel holding a Victorian lap desk; but after all, it was an antique, and the *Nouveau Voyage aux Isles de l'Amérique* a classic, and Julia had given them to me, and if she found out I'd left them behind, she might've felt hurt.

At the moonlit exit, the animal was gone; or rather he

was outside, with his tubular proboscis hanging down into the hole.

When I approached, the waiting nose retreated to give me room. Clutching my lap desk, I crept out of the burrow, to find myself in deepest jungle, in the middle of the night, surrounded by horrid nocturnal clickings, bloodcurdling bird screams, massive man-eating foliage, and nothing else.

I'd half a notion to dive back in the burrow, until my animal gave a sharp squeal and began a slow purposeful trot into the bush; having no better guide, I followed.

Where are we?

The animal clearly knew; it was on its own secret path through the forest, and I stumbled behind its fat bushy tail, waddling shape, and frequent encouraging squeaks; the trail soon grew so overlaid by vines and labyrmthine trees it was almost as dark as the burrow, and I had to get down on my hands and knees to navigate the tangled tunnel of leaves.

I could think of nothing I'd like less than following the footsteps of a vanishing beast, a project guaranteed to get me lost; but in what way could I consider myself found, no matter where I was, on this island? Better to follow an aimless porker than wait in a shack for my executioner. This was my one consolation—that though I had no idea where I was going, I was on my own.

Do *you* know where you're going? Does anyone know you are here? What a strange tortured path, etc. The philosophical implications were there, about man and his desert island where he finds his soul. I wanted only to find breakfast. I wanted my pain and mental anguish to abate, yes, but more than that I wanted a croissant. Or a brioche, filled with chocolate.

Was the beast gifted with rare optical rods, or simply a fabulous snout? It hurried on short churning legs through the black tropical thorn hedge as if skipping blithely along on the street where it was born.

I followed my pig as a blind man his dog, far from the eyes of my oppressors, deep into the island's wild interior where humans do not go—unless they are under two feet six. This was my escape through perilous divides. All traces of mankind fell away; we were in the solemn jungle; if an owl didn't carry me off, I might stand a chance.

For a person who finds a stroll through Abingdon Square exerting, our eight-legged race across the island was worse than a jog marathon. My snooting companion turned and looked my way: Was I coming?

What choice did I have? I felt like an ass trudging along on all fours, but it was preferable to carrying an ass, which is what I'd be doing if I'd stayed in the compound. Jungle shadows bid me be cautious; there were shrieks and cries from the leaves; I found myself muttering aloud, praying, chanting old favorite recipes: "Take one cup milk, two cups of flour . . ."

Plagued by mosquitoes and the most menacing sounds, hanging onto my unwieldy lap desk, clinging to a thin trail of squeaks in the night, I struggled through thick underbrush, panting loudly, flailing against branches and tendrils, tripping on roots, slipping in pools of sickening weed, muck, and mire, but always that short bushy tail was ahead of me, and I followed, desperately, feverishly, deliriously; where would the little cafe table be?

I wished for a thousand things, my tortured mind filled with fear; and yet it was filled with abandon too, because I was over the edge of the human world and into the vast darkness of the animals.

I'd resigned myself to crawling forever . . . when the blessed beast finally stopped.

We'd come to a cave of brush, a sort of bower, the creature's own den. I entered, collapsed in exhaustion, and thought of glowing hearths, of soft divans, oh God, how distant it all was and how little hope I had of seeing such things again.

That a Pluckrose should be sleeping with a pig seemed possible; Lord knows I'd slept in strange places, though this was indubitably the least comfortable. Squatting in the dark, crouched like a pygmy (but with far fewer resources), huddled at the end of nowhere with a porker, what had I accomplished? I'd merely postponed my demise—for what could I eat? How could I entertain myself?

What would become of me, in what manner would my downfall ensue? I might manage to find my way over a cliff, and death at the bottom; or be bitten by a snake or some monstrous spider, neither at all in my line. For the moment, the only thing between me and these dangers was the peculiar animal snoring beside me.

Sleep didn't come to me, though I counted gnats, counted centipedes' feet, and thrashed back and forth in the heat, an insect-riddled wreck. The bugs didn't seem to be biting the beast by my side, or his hide was remarkably thick. Night birds made ominous hooting sounds; I was shivering with fever and fear. (Or perhaps just fear. With trembling hand, I felt my brow. It was grimy but cool.) Oh, where is the U.S. Navy? (Or someone like that—a customs launch, a tourist boat.) Where are the forces of good?

The little beast next to me rolled over, wheezing contentedly in its slumber. Had it always been wild, or had it escaped from captivity? It seemed so tame and used to human company. Was it an escapee like me?

Two escaped figures hunched in the bush, as the night passed on interminable paws. Lizards appeared to be crawling over me. I felt a huge spider land on my nose. There seemed to be a toad on my elbow. And this, I knew, was only the beginning; my chances were decidedly poor.

But slowly, the ancient Pluckroses moved in my soul— from couch to café table, where they paused for a preparatory snack prior to going into action on my behalf.

There they are in the moonlight, gourmets all, in trailing robes of earlier days, dipping their fingers in the finger bowl of life once more, roused from eternal rest, and nearly ready for the terrible contest which lies ahead.

14

"You may call me Gregory," I said to the beast at breakfast, "and I shall call you Jean-Anthelme Brillat-Savarin."

I felt the great eighteenth-century gastronomist, if he were observing from heaven, would surely approve, so exquisite was the meal the animal served.

Imagine a delicacy somewhere between fresh truffles and buttered spring parsnips, imbibed on an empty stomach while reclining in a tropical bower of fern and liana on one's first morning of freedom; add to this a friendly bedfellow and the awareness that one might otherwise be bursting one's gut along with the vessels of one's only brain, and I think you'll have the full picture.

Naturally, the wonderful tubers Brillat-Savarin dug up and dished out lacked the penultimate refinements of washing and cooking, but it would've been gauche to pettifog.

Nor did I intend to share many more of these primitive, if charming, feasts with the beast. My plan was to steal a small boat at the first opportunity and putt-putt away to civilization.

"Monsieur Brillat-Savarin," I said, "thank you and adieu. If you will kindly point my way to the harbor, I won't impose on you further."

The creature, seeing me get up to leave, tucked its rubbery nose in my outstretched hand and offered a moist farewell snort.

"The same, I'm sure," I replied, noting a narrow pig-sized

path to my right, leading further up the mountain's summit; from there, I reasoned, I could get my bearings regarding the harbor.

There's a strange rain that falls in these mountains, so shimmery fine it barely alters the sunshine; you feel it merely as a welcoming coolness in the scorching dawn of the tropics. The higher you climb, however, the denser grows the mist, so that when you approach a summit, you enter another climate, a land invisible from below, a world where the island's perennial summer is veiled.

In my theatrical days I worked on *Brigadoon,* and had God's own time with the fog machine, defining the proper effect exactly mid pas de deux, so the heroine is wafted away to her secret world while the hero is left to leap about in crisply visible despair. Achieving the ethereal mist of the mountain peak, I rose from my four-legged position, lap desk tucked under arm, and glanced back down toward the path, still vivid and untouched by the rain clouds, and there was the animal—only a few yards behind me, but in another element.

The creature seemed spotlighted in radiance, its dark sloping back dazzled with sunbeams, its curious eyes softly gleaming, its lifted snout aglow like a fluorescent tube. So silent had been its footsteps, I didn't know until that moment the beast was tagging along.

Its devotion was all very flattering, but I had more important things on my mind. I turned my gaze in the other direction, where far down in the distance the glittering bay could be seen, and the crocodile-shaped cove, dotted with tiny white vessels and a large yellow destroyer.

Happily, Brillat-Savarin, or some other pig-sized animal, had beaten a second path down the mountain, in this bayward direction. I began my four-legged descent, a snuffling sound close at my heels.

The pig path followed the swampy bank of a river, beside which a tangled forest of bloodwood stretched great armlike roots, making the trail snakelike and writhing; one expected to be strangled by overhead vines or snatched into the swamp by the mad spreading roots of the bloodwood.

Mosquitoes clung to one's skin like a sucking suit of clothes. Orange-pronged blooms sprung up by our path, and crystal waterfalls; giant beetles with fearsome antennae whirred through the air like enemy helicopters; huge river crabs lifted hungry claws from the stream. The crickets were half a foot long, and from the terrifying resonance of their burps, the bullfrogs must've been big as six-month-old babies; there was also a sort of salamander dangling out of the trees, inflating its throat like a tangerine, and glaring hideously.

Even in such an atmosphere, crawling downhill goes faster than up; I presently drew near the harbor, where, for some reason, there were no sounds of activity.

Why, I wondered, aren't they buzzing back and forth from the destroyer in tenders? Where is everybody?

I crept to the edge of the woods and peered down to the water and docks. Directly below me an orange rubber dinghy was tied— with nobody in it, near it, or anywhere in sight. The boat was equipped with a small outboard motor; it was one of several such inflatable tubs belonging to the battleship; and I meant to have it.

A snort of excitement escaped the quivering snout of Brillat-Savarin.

"This is it," I said to the beast, and bid him a second farewell.

Cautiously glancing left and right, I heroically leapt off the bank and landed on all fours in the sand. No watchman's call answered my appearance on the beach; no guns began firing. I scrambled to my feet, gathered my lap desk, and clambered into the orange dinghy.

In a flash, I untied its rope.

I was off!

. . . Or would be as soon as I got the motor going. Any fool can start up an outboard; you turn the knob, pull the cord, and *zoom*. I've seen it done hundreds of times.

I turned the knob, pulled the cord, and shot straight out

to the wide-open sea . . . or, more specifically, straight into a coral reef ten yards away.

Coral reefs are not always visible to the above-water eye. This particular reef wasn't visible at all until it made its presence known by tearing the bottom out of my rubber boat.

With a terrible *glop-glop* sound, accompanied by the motor's death sizzle, my fleet progress was precipitously stopped and the boat went down.

I sank; I grabbed onto the boat; it sank; I grabbed onto the reef, which tore my hands and knees.

Death loomed, with its cinema replay of elegant rooms I'd designed, unforgettable meals I'd enjoyed, and fervent amours I'd lost, accompanied by the usual desperate prayers and obsequious promises to change my sinful ways.

Stunned as I was, immersed, and coral scraped, my floundering body, if not my panic-stricken brain, recalled how to swim, and since I was only ten yards from shore, survival was inevitable. I executed a few stunning side strokes (it's really the only style I'd advise when carrying a Victorian lap desk) and found myself once again sprawled on the beach—without boat, without hope, but alive, and ravenously hungry.

My ensemble of ragged silk slacks and ripped batik had received a much-needed rinsing, as had my foul person, but I feared for the delicate veneer of the lap desk and antique volume within, which I extracted to assess salt-water damage; Fielding's stitching and gluing held firm; the old Boy Scout's bindings were of the same indestructible mettle as their maker. Then I took out the little inkwell and quill to dry in the sun, followed by the tiny lid of the desk's secret compartment. Inside the secret compartment, to my amazement, lay the silver letter opener from L-port.

I was no longer unarmed.

But what, I asked myself in despair, ever made me think I could handle a boat? The one other time I'd been in charge of a vessel, its entire crew had been kidnapped.

On the bank the green bushes parted and the barrel

of a pistol pushed through, soon revealing itself to be Savarin's snout. I believe his curiosity about me intensified immeasurably after witnessing my unique performance with rubber tub. I mounted the bank and joined him. "Here I am, the proverbial bad penny."

He shoved me affectionately with his fat body, uttering several minor squeaks, which I was free to interpret as I saw fit.

Savarin (or someone like him) had bushwacked a satisfactory channel parallel to the road, and this is the tunnel of scrub I now crawled through, keeping well out of sight, lap desk tucked under arm.

When I arrived at the compound, there was still no one about.

Not even the guard dogs were there.

In a flash it came to me: They're all out searching for someone. And the last place they'll look for me is here.

Feeling quite like the purloined letter, I crept toward *el jefe's* villa, the lovely gabled structure I'd admired so often from prison; Savarin snuffled behind me across a crunchy white courtyard of shells, from which we made our way to the garden in back of the house.

Pale pink frangipani and florid hibiscus bordered a small citrus grove; stairs led to a dining porch suspended in a glade of bamboo. While the compound's inhabitants combed hill and dale for me with their hounds, I stealthily climbed the smooth steps, leaving Savarin to root in the orchard.

Low dining tables were covered with gay native cotton and set with bowls of cactus roses; wind chimes tinkled softly; I slipped through the doorway and entered the kitchen. To an aficionado of kitchens, it was more than acceptable:

Copper pots hung in profusion; pitchers bristled with wooden utensils; quiche and pâté molds decorated the walls. There were pantry and pastry alcoves, a six-burner stove with two ovens, Delft tiles, track lighting, and an admirable view of the orchard, this last feature embellished by Savarin's quaint, if vaguely prehistoric shape, digging up the vegetable garden.

I wasted not a moment—who knew when they might return? I set my lap desk down on the marble-topped counter, donned a frilly apron, and opened the refrigerator.

A wire basket of creamy brown eggs and some splendid red snappers decided me; I would create a snapper soufflé.

One might wonder at my confidence, attempting something so tricky as soufflé in an untried oven, but when the muse leads, the artist can only obey.

Humming Ravel's divine *Bolero,* I filleted my little fishies, seasoned them generously, cooked them (just barely) in butter, and laid them to rest in a medium-sized Pillivuyt soufflé dish. Through the screened window over my counter, I could see Brillat-Savarin enjoying some *haricots verts.*

If capture, torture, and death should come, I thought, let them arrive after I've eaten; saying this, I separated the eggs, grated some very nice Gruyere into the yolks, whipped the whites to a veritable volcano, folded all on top of the snappers, and slid the dish into the oven.

Is that the sound of a jeep approaching? No, it is merely my animal, snorting; he must have found a particularly delectable *haricot vert.*

The cellar stairs were housed in the pantry; I tripped down to pick out my wine. Once below, in the cold moldy vaults, I was in the classic position of rat in a trap but, as I suspected, the oenological selection was excellent, and I lingered so long in a tizzy of exquisite indecision that I finally feared for my soufflé, and settled for a simple Château Lafite, 1846.

Trilling the *Bolero,* I ascended with my dusty bottle, to discover by the celestial aroma that my soufflé was done.

What can I say? It was a soufflé to inspire a sonnet. I hung up my apron, and dined on the porch, in the shade of sweet-smelling ceiba, papaw, star apple, and mango, while Brillat-Savarin, in the vegetable garden below, made a meal of the remainder of the *haricot* row.

"My dear Anthelme," I called softly, toasting the odd-looking beast, "to your extreme longevity."

I couldn't help but feel that Savarin's longevity and mine

were directly related, since he'd gotten me this far, via his private tunnels aboveground and below.

I tottered back to the kitchen to ransack the refrigerator. Pushing aside a container of aspic jelly, I discovered—to my everlasting good fortune—a box of confections from the last factory in Zurich to make chocolates completely by hand. Armed with a tray of bonbons and 1846 Chateau Lafite, I made my way through the kitchen to a chamber the size of an airplane hangar, perfectly round, with a domed purple ceiling inscribed with the zodiac, mossy mauve carpeting, and the entire perimeter banked by a vast circle of pearl satin sofas. There was no other furniture, nor windows, but tiny lights and fans whirled overhead in the nighttime constellations.

I walked barefoot in my ragged clothing across the infinite mauve expanse, and sank with a cool satin sigh into the sofa of circular sofas.

Would they catch me? Would they kill me? I set my tray on the pearl fabric beside me, lifted a chocolate to my lips with unsteady fingers, and accidentally dropped one of the last handmade bonbons of Switzerland between the crack where the sectional connected. Greedily plunging my arm into the crevice to retrieve the lost piece of candy, my fingers struck some other protuberance . . . it felt like . . . a button.

The stars on the ceiling started to dim.

I gazed on in horror as the arc of wall opposite me opened and separated like the two halves of the world at Armageddon.

An enormous white screen slipped into the gap. The first scene of a Mexican movie started to roll, soundtrack booming.

Frantically I fumbled with the buttons.

The two halves of the earth ominously closed; the firmament above resumed its twinkling; the soundtrack fell silent.

I swallowed a medicinal mouthful of extreme vintage for my fluttering pulse.

For several long minutes I sat, breathlessly listening. No one came, so I reasoned no one had heard.

The room must be remarkably soundproof, or not one living soul is about in any part of the compound.

Wineglass in hand, I tiptoed from the video theater into what proved to be a more traditional living room, furnished in Chinese fretwork and a smattering of pre-Columbian, the baked-clay figures set in mirrored niches around encaustic walls.

The fretwork couches and chairs were upholstered alternately golf-links green and dandelion yellow—green, yellow, green, yellow, green, yellow, green, yellow, green, yellow, green, yellow. One could only stand appalled at *el jefe's* lack of judgment in refusing my professional services.

I quietly lifted a links-green chair and shifted it with a dandelion, so at least the alternating monotony was broken at one point in the room. I can't say it saved the day.

Shaking my head, I set my glass on the black polished surface of an utterly cliché fretwork table, and continued my prowling.

The central hall was richly paneled, its floor laid with faded Aubussons; elaborate plaster cornices and Louis Seize boiserie did much to offset the effect of unexceptional Tuscan chandeliers. My opinion was that the structure, in the right hands, had potential.

Mounting the stairs to the upper story, I straightened a Dubuffet on the wall. One couldn't help but feel the place appreciated a connoisseur's presence; it seemed to beckon me from chamber to chamber.

Misguidedly carried away, I flung my unwashed person on one luxurious bed after another, as if to consumer-test inner springs. The sight of my filthy imprint on a virginal white counterpane filled me with mortification.

I must, I saw, take a bath.

The master bath had been keenly influenced by the ladies' room at Radio City, or what one imagines that Deco den of hygiene to be. Mirror-stripped columns abounded; glass-and-chromium lamps stood everywhere; one could well imagine a dozen ample matinée matrons powdering their jowls during intermission, perched on a dozen baby-blue satin poufs.

My own sunken jowls were in drastic need of scraping. I located *el jefe's* shaving utensils, and razored with care. While waiting for the Jacuzzi to fill, I trimmed my dirty blond sideburns, cut my wretched toenails, brushed my bilious teeth, and generally made my person presentable.

One detests a skimpy bath. *El jefe's* tub was not skimpy. Having stirred in a handful of Crabtree & Evelyn crystals, I lowered myself into the water's warm fragrant depths; lolled; wallowed; splashed in the flowery steam; frolicked in the spray of the jets; lathered recklessly; and tossed sponges and louffas like so many juggling balls. It was infinitely more delightful than collapsing beneath a bale of marijuana, after which mules trod on one's face.

I'm ashamed to tell of the ring I left in that lovely tub, but it would've marred my voluptuous mood to get down on my knees with Bon Ami. And, practically speaking, I didn't think my life hung on the particular thread of whether or not I scrubbed *el jefe's* Jacuzzi before leaving.

He had some refreshing after-shave from Beverly Hills, with which I anointed, from topknot to toenail.

Washed, powdered, and expensively perfumed, I had quite the new lease on life. Placing such a clean body in filthy attire was out of the question.

I rummaged through *el jefe's* closets, trying this outfit and that, until I settled on simple silk underwear, white-embroidered Mexican shirt, and suit of ivory linen. My own foul clothing I neatly hung in the place of the ensemble I'd chosen.

From *el jefe's* bentwood hat tree, I selected a rakish Panama, then filled my pockets with Montecristo No. l's, borrowed a Cartier watch, and gazed at the vision I was: a Venezuelan murderer, of the better class.

If only my host's feet were my size. Unfortunately, I'd have to remain shoeless and sockless, the mysterious *el jefe* apparently being a gentleman of slender and elegant physique terminating in feet like those of a variegated hare.

Reborn, I strode through my villa and descended to the kitchen.

Donning my apron, I grated a couple of cucumbers (with peel, please). Add lemon juice, onion, salt, and pepper to taste, then proceed to the garden and pluck a fresh sprig of mint.

Savarin glanced up from his gorging. I think he approved my appearance. Above, the tropical sun smiled down.

To be brief, you must next chop the mint finely, add enough aspic for proper consistency, and place your soup in the refrigerator to set, which is where I left it for my host.

Moving soundlessly on pink manicured feet, I returned to the Louis Seize hallway and made my way to the farther wing.

I entered a very attractive chamber, a place of extreme intimacy, designed for solitary pleasures, with only a narrow, pillow-laden opium bed, a round copper stand, and a small Chagall on the wall. I automatically straightened the painting, only to discover it covered a tiny window; glancing through the window, I found myself looking into another room.

This second room was a library, lined with cork, bookshelves, and dark draperies. Maps of the world studded with colored pushpins decorated the gloomy panels. Maroon leather wing chairs and green glass reading lamps predominated, along with a massive writing table, behind which sat a wizened old man in a size 36-short linen suit.

My immediate impression—though obviously hallucinatory— was that his arms were red to the elbow, steeped in blood. His face was brown and wrinkled as a discarded grocery bag, and intensely intelligent in the most horrifying way; his hair was straight and black, perhaps dyed; his hands, like his feet, were disproportionately large, twitching like two Venus flytraps, as the old man's terrible eyes stared up at the map nearest him.

I stood frozen at the window, then dumbly followed my

frightened feet backward, out of the charming little room. My soufflé fell within me as will the soufflé of a woman in love collapse instead of rising in the oven.

Weak in will and knee, I fled through the green and yellow salon, back through the lavender cinema, to the kitchen. I gathered my lap desk and hurried out to the garden.

"Run for your life," I called to my animal.

But Savarin was munching an aubergine.

He eyed me with half-cocked snout and continued his meal.

I begged; I pleaded. "These people shoot gophers for nibbling one beet green. What do you think they'll do to a prehistoric pig who's dug up half the garden?" (In a sense, I exaggerated; I'd never actually seen anybody shoot gophers, but one can fairly safely assume that an old gentleman with arms red to the elbows in human blood is not a founding member of the Fund for Animals.)

I continued to urge Savarin to leave his eggplant; the beast refused to be budged. Nor would he lead me to safety until he'd swallowed every last morsel, and only then, when he'd had his fill, did he slowly waddle out of the compound, I behind him on the knees of *el jefe's* ivory suit.

15

LIBERATED BY A SNUFFLING BEAST, I LIE AT NIGHT in our bower, and reflect on freedom, the sweetest of sweetmeats.

I embrace snoozing Savarin.

"You are the finest pig in the world," I say in a straightforward way. He opens his bright beady eyes, and we watch the stars pass above us as the night goes by.

From whence does this affection spring?

There is an agreement, perhaps, on vegetables, their preparation and the manner in which one eats them, an appreciation of *nouvelle cuisine.*

Of what does Savarin dream? What succulent tubers drift through his sleep? He sighs, rolls over.

The dawn comes finally, and finds me up and about, bathing in a clear jungle stream. I feel quite refreshed and could enjoy a *Times;* if there were coffee, it would be an absolute tropical idyll.

Instead, I peruse Père Labat, who indicates that I am probably coming down with *la maladie de Siam.* While reading poetic descriptions of yellow fever (*"My temperature was so high, they thought I was on the eve of a voyage for which no ship would be necessary."*—P. Labat), I nibble a few berries, some bark.

Savarin duly appears, a large mango held in his teeth.

"Dear creature," I say, devouring the fruit.

In the distance, guns fire.

Just the thing to ruin a tropical idyll.

And so begins a typical day . . .

I walk through my jungle, its aroma now familiar, its vines and spiders no longer alarming. It seems I've adjusted, as I've done so many times in my life. There's nothing hardier than a human being at his wit's end; underneath our frail facade, we're a tough and adaptable species. I know therefore I can hold out, but also that I'll eventually grow bored; my plan is to flee the island before it comes to that point. (In love affairs too I find this is best, that one sail away before passion's flower ripens into routine.)

My schemes form as I root with Savarin for our lunch. I dream of a raft of sticks on which to float off—but this doesn't seem sound. I consider stealing another lifeboat—but the people in the compound are so sensitive about their possessions.

We crawl on through the bush. Over the days, I've discovered that Savarin's network of verdant passages spans much of the island, and, after some trials, I've identified the main ones, naming them after the boulevards of Paris.

The Boulevard St. Germain led to the marijuana farms in the low-lying hills, where the cash crop was harvested by fine-boned, handsome natives, who practiced innovative economics by padding the weight of the bales with mule dung; I noticed one creative employee with high achievement motive toss a dead rat into the mixture, bespeaking a nice contempt for both the Stateside distributor and the great American consumer; that man, I perceived, is management potential.

After watching the farmers, Savarin and I strolled along the Boulevard Raspail in the direction of Montparnasse and the jungle heights. We knelt at the stream for a drink, and I pondered my options, gazing down through rain-shimmered forest; as my eyes grew used to the mist, I made out the antlike forms of the rebels, swarming from the branches of trees far below, their mortar shells thudding dully in the ravine.

We crept closer, the better to spy . . .

Good God, there is Sissie, in camouflage fatigues and one of those dreadful hats with a curtain in back.

I stared amazed at her *zaftig* profile climbing through obstacle courses, swinging on ropes, hurling grenades, and performing any number of barbarous acts. She seemed admirably fit for the practice. One could only reflect on good breeding and sadly conclude that the dear girl never had any.

I nudged my animal to turn and ascend the boulevard.

He ascended perhaps fifty yards, then sniffed the ground with excitement, suddenly veered, and charged into a small clearing, where he began to feverishly root.

I knew the symptoms too well. Savarin, that incorrigible gourmet, had sensed the presence of unusually fine tubers.

"This is neither the time nor the place," I whispered.

As if deaf, the beast went on digging.

Like his great namesake, the first Brillat-Savarin, who strode into court in full magistrate wig, a brace of freshly killed partridge dangling from his waist to keep them warm with his own body heat for supper later that evening, Savarin the Second put first things first, the very first being his stomach.

What was one to do? Leave a helpless animal to the firing squad, or make the job go faster by pitching in?

I looked around nervously and fell to work beside him, digging in the soft dirt until my fingernails hit something hard; I sat up with a curse. "Rocks, you poor fool, we're digging on ledge."

With a squeak of triumphant disagreement, Savarin tugged out a plump whitish tuber.

"Oh, all right." I resumed my digging, next to the ledge, which seemed to be strangely confined to a narrow space, where it plunged straight down like an underground wall.

"Qu'est-ce que c'est que ça?"

Getting no reply from Savarin, I satisfied my curiosity by clearing out the earth on top of and surrounding the straight-sided rock. Covered and embedded with soil, my rock didn't reveal its true nature for several seconds.

The object was, in fact, an enormous stone crock.

Now it was I who worked furiously, wiping the dirt from the crock's large heavy lid, which was stuck tight from its time underground and came off only with difficulty.

Shades of Pandora. My feelings were decidedly mixed; the buried crock might hold a bomb which would blow me to *Streusel* or, at the other extreme, ninety-six back issues of my favorite magazine.

Savarin glanced at my discovery, sniffed, and returned to his truffling. The crock contained several big leather sacks bound with rawhide, clearly not up the beast's culinary alley.

Bombs? Surely not.

Copies of the *Digest?* Much too heavy.

I untied the crumbling rawhide of the topmost satchel and peeled back the dry leather collar.

Rarely have I been so at a loss for the *mot juste*. To be perfectly frank, I babbled like a brook.

In the satchel were coins. Heaps and heaps. Not nickels and quarters but, rather, coins of long ago, from what might've been every mercantile nation on earth in that distant era. It was a veritable numismatic museum: round coins, square coins, octagonal coins, large coins and small coins, thick coins and wafer-thin coins, and all of them, gold coins.

It's amazing what wealth will do.

Even more than snapper soufflé and a hot Jacuzzi.

Confidence surged through my veins like cocaine; I was no longer just another out-of-work decorator, but a gentleman of independent means.

If I wished, I might start my own classic, founded-on-piracy, great American dynasty.

I might become a raving philanthropist.

I might abandon the ranks of professionals and become an amateur.

Assuming, of course, that all my bags held the same glittering treasure.

This assumption soon proved wrong. Every sack I opened held the rarest gold coins, except for the last, which was bursting with diamonds of flawless blue, rubies of archaic dimension, emeralds from Colombia, and pearls of that rather vomitive pink which forms once in a thousand conch shells and is usually traded by the diver who finds it for his own fishing boat business.

"My dear Savarin," I said humbly.

Again and again, this ill-featured creature had proved to be my benefactor. Yet he demanded neither gratitude nor glory, but was content to snuffle at my unwashed heels, put up with my abominable ignorance, and listen to endless boastful tales from my past.

I removed the leather sack of jewels and returned the others to their hiding place; their weight was too great for me to carry more than one bag per trip. Carefully, I recovered the crock and raked leaves and debris on top of the earth, then made mental note of the exact address and respectfully asked Savarin whether or not he was ready to burrow on home.

We had barely gotten into the leafy tunnel, Savarin foremost, and I bringing up the rear with my sack of gems, when a volley of bullets whistled over our heads.

A loud squeal rose from Savarin, who took off on short churning legs, while I set a new speed record for the four-hundred-meter dash through thorn hedge.

Bullets whizzed about us. This is too much, I thought, hurtling along in four-legged fashion, my heavy leather satchel swinging from my teeth and what was left of my bridgework.

What I feared most was flamethrowers, but apparently our pursuer didn't have any. When I thought I'd gained time, I made the mistake of Lot's wife and turned around to see— not the city of Sodom, but Sissie, struggling awkwardly through the bush, wielding a submachine gun Gregory-ward.

Oh, that Sissie, I thought in exasperation, doubling the speed of my scuttling, she's so impressionable.

Another round of bullets flew toward me.

And she never had any taste.

To think of the endless ha-ha's I'd sat through, the idiotic political speeches, the offensive theological opinions; to think that I'd worried about the girl like a mother and actually gave her my own boiled tarantula.

The look I'd seen in her eyes spoke ancient enmity; she'd always loved tormenting me; and she was *so* athletic.

Thank goodness she didn't have my experience plowing four-footed through pig roads; Savarin and I were able to keep well ahead of her fire.

When suddenly the animal veered.

"Please, Savarin, not now."

The incorrigible gourmet disappeared from sight. I automatically followed his lead, the last glimpse of his westbound tail, and found myself tumbling, sack foremost, into a pit.

I lay face down on my treasure in a hole in the ground, awaiting execution, accompanied by a five-hour harangue, and followed by on-the-spot burial.

A wet rubber nose touched my face. Above us, and slightly eastward, we heard the thundering bootsteps of Sissie pursuing us along the Boulevard Raspail; she raged through the brush, shooting wildly, in chase of a will-o'-the-wisp; and gradually the sound of her fury faded. True, I was deep in a vile hole, some kind of native animal trap, but I'd eluded the firing squad.

We lay shoulder to shoulder and waited for the dreadful girl to give up and go home. I stirred jewels with the tips of my fingers and reflected on life in a burrow; it seemed to offer distinct advantages.

Sissie's footsteps never returned.

Toward evening, I decided she must've gotten lost, or met up with the jeep road; in any case, we were safe.

"Forgive me, old man," I said to Savarin, picking him up and heaving him unceremoniously over the rim of the pit; my bag of jewels followed; I, being taller than any animal the trap was designed for, merely crawled up and out, and so we resumed our homeward design, via the Boulevard Raspail, the Rue de Vaugirard and, at last, the Place de l'Odéon.

Our little apartment in the Odéon, though disgusting and

crawling with beetles, was doubly sweet to me that evening.
I deposited my sack in the innermost bower, vowing to go
back the next morning and dig up the rest of the treasure.

The tropical moon rose high in the sky, with *el jefe's*
horrible face inside it; I seemed to see his wizened features
in the wrinkled mountains looming around us and hear
his might in the rumble of the military. His fleet was
protected, the island hills were protected, and it would take
a considerable army to dislodge him.

My plans for outwitting the island's ruler were more
humble. I wished only to escape with my hide, and several
million in treasure; challenge enough for an interior
decorator.

Night also brought visions of Manitou, the Carib god
of evil, and meditations on sundry witchcraft ceremonies
detailed by Father Labat. So vivid were his culinary
descriptions of how to preserve the limbs of slain enemies
(rendered fat is best placed in a large gourd for transport)
and antiwitchcraft remedies (remove victim's heart, burn in
quick lime), I was beginning to regret not having let the
good priest drown in the ocean.

But Savarin was the best of companions.

As the stars slowly passed overhead, along with the
horrible face of *el jefe,* as tanks rumbled and sorcerers
prowled,^ lay next to that excellent animal and whispered
soothing words in his ear.

". . . and then there was the adobe villa I did in Ravello,
above the Gulf of Salerno, the most serendipitous wedding of
pure eleventh century and Bauhaus. Imagine, if you will, six
tubular Mies side chairs set off by Roman arches. *Gregory,*
said the princess, *only an absolute genius . . .*" Etc. Etc. Etc.

16

Jungle madness, I thought to myself; I felt it was somewhat like the famed cabin fever, but infinitely worse.

We were taking our stroll through the bush (on all fours), and I was dreaming of life in the city—any city—even the dullest city in the world. I thought of dull cities I have known, and even the deadliest of them (Muncie, Indiana, *par exemple),* boasted a certain freedom from mosquitoes on Main Street.

In a manner of speaking, Savarin had solved the problem of bugs. As a gourmet and *bon vivant,* he could not suffer the bother of bites, but made a habit of rolling in a moist herb which repelled insects. I, seeing his example and its effects, did likewise. However, this meant I was always covered in odoriferous herb.

I took solace in a waterfall bath, but even that delicious experience served to point up the bitter absence of a large fluffy bath towel. Would I ever again enjoy the clean friction, the warm well-being, the freshly laundered favors of pure cotton terry?

True, the state I was in was better in every way than prison, but mucking around in the mangroves is hardly one's idea of boulevardiering. Where were the elegant shops? Where the carefree cafés? Where the cosmopolitan crowds?

Savarin, of course, was splendid, waddling along like some minister of the court in the First Empire, a wholesome sight for any put-upon decorator; the good animal brightened up the horizon, of which there was now a considerable portion, as we attained the top of the mountain.

I reached the summit and gazed at the sea. Like stout Cortez, I stood silent upon a peak in Darien and thought of Bloomingdale's.

For a long time I watched the tiny boats come and go in the distance, until the thudding of hoofbeats shocked me back to my senses; I flung myself on my belly in the brush and saw—not twenty feet from the pig path we'd taken—a gorgeous golden stallion charging up the mountain, bearing a majestic yellow-robed figure.

The plateau, as I've indicated, gave out on a dizzying vista of the bay; so it seemed, from my hiding place, as if the tall figure in yellow, astride the galloping stallion, was riding out of his own battleship, the daffodil-dyed vessel of war dominating the blue cove below. At that moment I knew I could never again in life think of the sheik as anything but the Destroyer.

Before the dust had settled in his wake, a trio of bodyguards appeared on three black horses, escorting the Destroyer on his mission. Here, for some reason unknown, Savarin uttered a series of hysterical squeals and waddled out of the woods onto the bridle trail behind the horses. Only the sound of hooves covered his squeals; I ran out and snatched the deluded creature up in my arms.

"Are you insane?" I demanded, taking cover again with my beast in the brush.

His reply was to trundle along the thorn hedge, after the enemy, as if devoured by curiosity.

"As long as you keep low in the bush," I admonished him, following on hands and knees across the plateau and down the other side of the mountain, "and muffle your ridiculous voice."

I admit that I too was curious.

Was the Destroyer bound for a rendezvous?

With whom?

My first thought was of Sissie—romance—but I should've known: A Destroyer has no heart.

His rendezvous was with Colonel Goose-step.

They sat on two rocks by the stream, in a glade, the golden-robed Arab and the medal-festooned commander.

Savarin and I huddled well in the brush and listened to words which made my hair stand on end.

I regret I wasn't close enough to follow the entire scenario, a catalogue of aggression, penetration, and destabilization in what sounded like every troubled nation that had recently edged onto the world stage, as well as some which hadn't yet exploded. The conversation was riddled with initials, each string of letters a clandestine operation in what was apparently a thrust at global dominion.

A cold feeling of menace descended like mist from the hills. It seemed I was watching an age-old game that is always the same, its object always power, its weapon fear, its current curriculum consisting of small, independent armies, out of which a world leader can rise, as did Schickelgruber, from the ranks of gangsters.

A revolutionary enterprise was unfolding before my eyes, and it was clearly my patriotic duty to stop it.

Unless, of course, the revolutionaries were ours.

How was one to distinguish CIA from KGB, PLO, IRA, etc.? The difference appeared subtle.

I was sweating profusely and Savarin was shivering. The lovely forest glade where two men lounged on rocks and a beautiful gold stallion grazed seemed to exhale vapors of unbreathable evil. I feared I would suffocate on a poison that thickened the air but was invisible and nonanalyzable by any chemical test.

At last, the Destroyer mounted his horse and bid Colonel Goose-step good-bye, his dark eyes resting on the soldier with a coldness which was profound. I believe I've mentioned that when the Destroyer entertained us on his yacht, on a long-ago day in the Virgins, one sensed a certain distance between him and the rest of humanity; this distance seemed, in the intervening weeks, to have widened until it was a black hole in the universe.

Savarin squeaked.

The Destroyer glanced in our direction but gave no sign of seeing any more than the usual ferns, lianas, and showy hibiscus. He uttered a guttural command, which produced his bodyguards from the far side of the glade, and the four tall riders thundered down the mountain.

Colonel Goose-step sat and stared at the stream, his fleshy features marked by the peculiar passage of his thoughts, as pine trees are twisted and distorted by cruel ocean winds. *Enfin,* he gave the same shudder-inducing smile he'd given in the hut, and off he marched, hup two, hup two.

Savarin and I crept home to our bower in a sorry state; the encounter had made me nauseous and dizzy and I couldn't stop my hands from trembling. Though I knew the poison I'd swallowed was merely mental, it had produced the same panic flow through my veins that injesting cyanide might.

We lay in our flowery cave, and I made feeble attempts at cheerful normality.

". . . The entire stairwell was glass. Everyone loved it . . ."

But even a fulsome account of the famous mirrored staircase I'd designed for some very dear friends in the Dakota didn't lift our spirits, as it certainly should have.

And then the grenade fell.

Not quite on our heads, but close enough for Savarin to immediately set to the most furious digging, his ubiquitous solution to all of life's problems: *Go deeper.*

I knew, of course, the villain was Sissie, hunting us personally, and what angered me most was that she would bomb not just me, but Savarin.

How loathsome.

I could imagine her motives, all of them low.

She wanted to impress the revolutionaries, perhaps win a silly medal to pin on her silly campaign hat.

I lay, with Savarin frantically uprooting the floor of our home, and waited while Sissie bracketed us with grenades, and then the bracketing moved away, off in another direction; she'd found the general area of our hideout, but not the exact spot.

This persecution of an innocent animal was not to be tolerated.

I might not be able to save the world, but I could at least defend my own pig (or whatever he was).

I made my decision, and laid my plans.

17

THE HIGH HILLS BECAME MINE.

Every minute I could spare from foraging (a program which took more time than you'd think, as Savarin would eat only the best tubers and truffles, forty-five dollars the ounce), I spied and awaited my chance.

I learned the militia's schedules, their routines, their habits; such a boring crowd of roughnecks. I checked out the beaches on the quiet side of the island, and collected bits of jetsam—broken crates, plastic bags, oil cans, bottles, and rope; I salvaged every scrap, piling my stores in a grotto beside a shallow inlet, a cove too shallow for boats to navigate and therefore relatively private.

It was to this grotto that I hauled my seven sacks of treasure, along with my lap desk. Our former apartment in the Odeon was no longer safe after sundown, when Sissie pursued her private manhunt; during the day she was busy training, and it was during the day I would attack.

Between one and two in the afternoon, the rebel road by the Boulevard du Montparnasse was rarely used; around two, Sissie walked by briskly; at two-fifteen or two-twenty, Colonel Goose-step crossed in the opposite direction. From two-thirty on, the militia had lunched and digested, and the rest of their day was spent thrashing about.

It was drizzling slightly when I set to work, exactly at one (so kind of *el jefe* to lend me his Cartier watch). Savarin stood guard, snooting around, while I shinnied up a tall spindly palm tree, a feat

I'd been perfecting for several excrutiating days. Needless to say, if three months previous you'd told me I would soon be a counterin-surgent on a tropical island, one interior decorator against an entire rebel army, swinging from trees like a long-tailed lemur, I would have cocked a skeptical eyebrow.

I tied one end of my rope to the top of the trunk, utilizing a clove hitch. My tree seemed to sway like a flute-loving cobra in lazy counterpoint to the undulating jungle and footpath far below, where the snooting figure of Savarin looked tiny indeed, a miniature tapir adrift on a rolling green sea.

I shut my eyes to regain composure and balance, and slowly shinnied down; I believe it's commonly thought that return trips are shorter than going, but this particular descent took an unconscionable time.

I fastened two clamps in the ground, one on either side of the road, threading the rope through the clamp directly under the tree; then, using this clamp as a lever, I tugged until the palm was bent double. (Not in vain had I sat through dozens of Saturday afternoon serials in my culturally twisted childhood, stuffing my juvenile face with chocolate nonpareils and a particularly loathsome candy that came on a long strip of paper in the form of colored dots, which you bit off, glue included.)

I looped the rope in the road, noose fashion, then threaded it through the second clamp and covered the loop, as had Tarzan, or someone of his ilk, with the good earth.

Ready for the main feature to begin, I took my seat in the bushes and could practically taste the candy glue. There was time for several cartoons, a couple of newsreels, and a good popcorn fight before my fair foe stepped into view.

The motto of the Pluckrose family is, *We offer beauty, but you must beware of our thorns.*

I'd suffered Sissie's insults long enough in flowerlike sweetness; now Pluckrose of the Jungle would strike.

It all happened so fast I could barely savor the action; in one moment she was walking briskly, her ample bosom crisscrossed with ammunition, and in the very next instant she was dangling thirty feet in the air from one ankle.

In her upending, three things had tumbled—her absurd desert hat with the curtain in back, her binoculars, and her submachine gun.

Before she could scream, I had the submachine gun pointed upward.

"One word, and I'll blow you to bits," I hissed.

If she'd had any sense at all, she should've known it was bluff—I mean, would *you* know how to work a submachine gun?—but I suppose the sight of a pointed weapon, viewed when dangling upside down from one's ankle, tends to be impressive. For once in her horrid life, the booby was speechless.

Much as I enjoyed the sight of my enemy hanging like this, her strawberry hair streaming earthward away from her upside-down blood-red face, I hadn't time to waste.

"Let's have the rest of the ammunition."

I saw her hesitate, eyes blazing, but she was not in a position to argue, and she struggled to unbuckle the bandoleers. "You'll be sorry for this," she croaked hoarsely, "Gregory Pluckrose."

"But Sissie dear, I thought you'd be thrilled to see how physically fit I've become. Now take off your shirt, and throw it down too."

It didn't compare with *el jefe's* white-on-white Mexican, being patterned with some idiot's idea of brown and green leaves, but I needed a change for laundry day. She unbuttoned her shirt with difficulty, disengaged her arms, and flung down the garment. "I'll have you begging for death," she hissed.

"I dreamt I was a revolutionary in my Maidenform bra," I replied without pity. "And your trousers."

"How the hell can I take off my pants with a rope round my ankle, you nincompoop."

I saw her point. Ditto for the boots.

"If you promise to be nice," I said, "I might let you down." The dreadful girl spat on my head; her aim was superb.

Yet how aesthetically restful it was to a person of taste to see Sissie hanging in silence, sans funny stories, sans grace, sans political ravings. "You'll curse the day you were born," she gasped in a strangled voice.

"Why? Are you planning to take out my appendix?"

I glanced at my Cartier, regretted I had no time to linger, and gathered my booty, slinging as much as I could round my body— ammunition belt, jungle knife, submachine gun. *Pluckrose,* I said, *you are definitely a man in possession of himself*

"Goose-step will be along in five minutes," I told Sissie. "If you scream before then, I'll come back and blow off your bra."

On this note, I turned with my animal and dove into the Boulevard du Montparnasse, which we followed for just a short while, then cut off toward the Luxembourg Gardens, and the numerous side streets of the Quarter, until none but a native Parisian could possibly trace our route's convolutions.

I had certain fleeting compunctions about leaving Sissie hanging upside down in her underwear, but never let guilt interfere with healthy, natural, and well-aimed hatred. This was my philosophy, recently arrived at, after the girl tried to bomb me to bits. Kindness is all very well, but Sissie had gone beyond my love; so she was left up a tree, as the saying goes.

That night, the hills echoed with explosions; not just Sissie was now on my trail, but the entire militia. *What kind of rebel army are we,* they must've asked themselves, *if we can't take a single decorator?*

The next morning, in our grotto, I awoke sopping wet.

And thoroughly depressed.

Life in the bush, in the pouring rain, I realized, is intolerable.

True, I was free, in a manner of speaking, and rich, but what had I to look forward to?

. . . According to Father Labat, either being pierced with a barbed poisoned arrow; clubbed on the head; hammered to mash and strangled; burned alive; hung up to rot in a cage; or threshed through a sugar-cane mill—depending on who caught me. (Not to mention being soaked through with rain. I was ready to risk all for another hot bath.)

I gazed at my pile of junk. What good were my water jugs, Baggies, and nautical rope, when I didn't possess the skill even to paddle a raft?

. . . provided I could construct a raft which didn't sink on contact with water,

. . . and then provided I could point it in the proper direction.

No, I'd been deluding myself.

My future was tubers.

What wouldn't I give to have one decent meal on a table set with a few white camellias in a simple Favrile vase?

Beside me tropical blossoms were exploding with moisture and brilliant color and I was practically sleeping in a bed of orchids; but it wasn't the same.

I was in need of the finer things—some Rosenthal china and a cup of Formosa oolong.

I was prepared to fight every mercenary on the island for an issue of *Connoisseur* magazine, served up with scones and Lap-sang souchong.

I lay in the rain and dreamt of all these things, all that I loved, all that made life meaningful; and, slowly, my courage rose.

Slowly, I girded myself for battle with the powers that ruled the island.

Pluckrose of the Jungle would triumph, for the sake of a slice of something exquisite in the way of cake.

I would work my will on this lost isle of outlaws.

I would rescue the one man who could sail a raft through the Caribbean without compass, rudder, or radar.

I would rescue Albion.

18

THE QUESTION WAS: WOULD THAT DUCK-BILLED mariner throw in with me? I thought of his grizzled face and wondered whether I even wanted the demented old bird along. But he could maneuver a boat; which I could not.

So I crept toward *el jefe's* compound under cover of darkness, disguised as a mercenary, in Sissie's hat and shirt and *el jefe's* now filthy pants. Around my neck hung binoculars; across my chest were strapped bandoleers; in my hand was Sissie's submachine gun.

Savarin skulked in the lead. The tropical night was filled with drums and explosions, the songs of birds and insects, and the sound of human voices which came from afar and faded.

I would get the old salt to join me, and free darling Julia. Poor woman—degraded, mind failing from overexposure, her fortune lost, a plaything of pirates—she needed her decorator's touch to bring her back to her senses, back to security and well-chosen furniture, such as a seat in the boat I would somehow obtain to carry us away.

She was in a tropical frenzy, this I knew; she needed to be cooled and soothed. She had been good to me and I would repay her, no matter what the cost—so long as I wasn't likely to be poached *a l'anglais;* or boned, baked, and served on *balisier* leaves; either of which was a possibility, but certain chances must be worth taking.

Mustn't they?

Our leafy tunnel led to the Pont de la Concorde, whose

exposed ramparts we'd have to cross before reaching the more fashionable arrondissements.

On the Quai Anatole France, we entered the moonlight. Standing erect, I moved stealthily forward. To my horror the trees ahead of me separated; Savarin squeaked; and a man stepped toward us.

I lifted my submachine gun, squeezed the foregrip, yanked the trigger . . .

And nothing happened.

I proceeded to pull every lever, of which there were many, but none of them produced so much as a peep or a BB.

The man came closer.

I yanked the trigger so hard I lost my footing and sank in a sweat to the ground as the thundering silence of my marksmanship echoed around me.

"Hey, mon, you okay?"

I gazed up from my swoon to see a concerned black face. A hellish knife hung from the waist of my would-be victim's shorts, but otherwise he was naked.

Savarin had darted back into the bush—perhaps with reason, if the man with the knife was out hunting nocturnal animals of the rooting, burrowing, plumpish variety.

The hunter smiled in the most cordial way and offered me his hand; I rose unsteadily with his help.

"Full moon, sick fall," quoth he sympathetically, putting the kindest possible interpretation on my display of nonshooting prowess; or maybe he actually believed the full moon had felled me. In any event, I was terribly relieved that I hadn't figured out how to use Sissie's submachine gun. Suppose I'd shot this amiable gentleman? The very thought made me ill.

"You soldier boss," he grinned. "Sure bet."

From which I inferred he approved of the military.

"*El jefe,* dot my mon," he informed me. "Best ting hoppen to dis island. Progress for de people. Give everybody job, here, dere, on de pock train."

I recalled the face of the stricken driver as he collapsed beneath his bale, fate unknown. The moon slanted its rays on my companion's strong features; here was an islander, friendly toward soldiers, believing me to be one; here was a source of information.

Casually, I inquired, "Has *el jefe* lived here long?"

"Dot mon? Live here? Not big mon like *el jefe*. On dis little island? Ha-ha. Dis just his businessmon's vacation."

His businessmon's vacation? Then this huge drug operation with fleets of ships, teams of natives, and international armies was just a refreshing sideline, a bit of a hobby to keep his mind occupied while relaxing. What must his main business be?

I swaggered arrogantly in the moonhght, patting my hand grenade. What were spooky jungle sounds and shooting stars to a mercenary?

"Before *el jefe*," went on the historian, "dis island one big noting. Every mon had a Bible. Every womon had de long dress. Everybody had de vaccination. No one allowed to chew leaf. Den comes *el jefe*. Progress for de people. Every mon trow de Bible in de bay. Every womon trow dress in de ocean. No more vaccination. Everybody chew leaf. *El jefe*, him trow de missionary in de sea."

"He shipped them out?"

"Ha-ha. Sure bet. Out to de sharks. Now everybody prosper."

"Does everybody," I asked casually, "prefer *el jefe* to the missionaries?"

"Always some troublemaker," he admitted with a deprecatory wave of his hand. "But *el jefe* take care of dem. You want to see skeletons?" he asked eagerly.

"Some other time perhaps," I replied, with a bold swagger-in-moonlight to indicate it wasn't squeamishness that kept a killer like myself from admiring skeletons.

"Sure bet." He seemed disappointed, but resigned to accept that I was too busy with important matters for his skeletons; his manner was disturbingly respectful, as if I'd impressed him tremendously. Possibly, he felt that every thief and criminal in *el jefe's* army was a prominent statesman and leader of justice.

"Do government boats ever come here?" I inquired, in a manner implying I desired to turn my submachine gun on every last one of them for target practice. "Coast guard? Police?"

"In de old day. Before de progress. Now *el jefe* shoot de police right out of de water." He pointed to the top of a tree and grabbed his neck with brutal fierceness; his eyes rolled up in his skull, his tongue lolled out of his mouth. When he'd finished his realistic pantomime, the poor fellow was gasping piteously.

"*El jefe* hangs policemen?"

"Sure bet." His eyes lit up. He reached into his shorts and drew out a flat leather wallet, which opened to reveal a small blue-and-brass customs badge and an identity card for one Guillermo Jesus Manuel Cordero.

The late Guillermo Jesus was a hirsute individual of indeterminate youth, with an effete and fatuous expression and rather surprisingly pale skin and eyes. I studied the photo and particulars for such a long time that at last the wallet's present owner grew nervous. "Me no steal, mon."

"How did you get it?"

"Me no know."

"Did you take it from the hanged man?"

He shook his head vigorously. "Me no steal, mon. You no tell *el jefe* me steal." His eyes changed from frightened to sly. "You want?"

I slipped the wallet into my pocket. "Sure bet."

A smile of relief spread over his features, so glad was he to escape the punishment meted to those who steal from *el jefe,* even if it meant he had to give up his treasure. He pumped my hand with emotion, an emotion which was shared; I couldn't help thinking that if things had turned out differently, he might've been singing of *my* sacrifice in de moonlight. For that matter, he still might.

Eager to change the subject from his suspicious possession of the customs man's wallet, he asked, "You know de lady rebel who has swore by her yellow hair to catch de foe of her heart and boil him in coconut oil?"

"Intimately," I replied. "I'm off right now to help her catch him and assist with the boil."

"Be careful, mon." The native lowered his voice fearfully. "Him great jungle fighter. Him master of obeah and ruler of de pigs; him put a spell upon de pigs so dey must help him."

I glanced quickly behind, to make sure Savarin was concealed in the bush.

"Him has magical name," whispered the native. "Him de judgment of higher power. Him door opener, who make de spell to pass through de door. Him pass into de house of *el jefe* and take all *el jefe's* clothes while everybody dere." His voice trembled with veneration and awe. "And den him pass into de kitchen and cook up all de food for a hundred people and eat it himself."

This last *coup de cuisine* impressed him the most. "Only a mon who sell his soul to de devil could eat dot much food."

"And the lady rebel?" I inquired.

"De most bloodtirsty womon ever come to dis island." He performed an enthusiastic charade to show she was also expert with explosives. "Bang! Bang! Bang!"

One sensed admiration. He beckoned my ear to his lips; in an almost inaudible whisper he confided that she was actually the Queen of Sweden.

From this well of camaraderie he took me totally into his confidence and began to explain in heartfelt terms the basis of his profound respect for *el jefe* and progress.

"In de old day, de river flow down de hill everywhere. But we too stupid, we only drink and wash in dere. Den come *el jefe,* and drive de river into every mon's hut." His words throbbed with emotion. "De sink. De bathtub. De W.C. Dis is what *el jefe* give to my people."

I appreciated his deep feeling. It was all I could do to resist rushing home with the excellent fellow and plunging into his wonderful, progressive, gravity-fed bathtub.

But I had another errand.

I clicked my feet, saluted, gave a vague *heil jefe,* and bid my new friend farewell; he went his way and I mine, like ships that pass in the night on the Seine.

Savarin waddled out of the thicket. I studied him carefully for evidence that he realized he was bewitched by a master of obeah and door opener.

With no sign of subservience, he led me down the trail in the direction of *el jefe's* compound, and I dutifully followed. I, who should be shopping at Bloomie's, was Lord of the Jungle and King of the Pigs, mucking about in the hills with an automatic rifle (or something) which I couldn't figure out how to fire. I made another attempt to pull the trigger, but succeeded only in exhausting myself. Nor could I get the pin out of the hand grenade strapped to my belt.

The tropical wind moved through the trees; the useless hand grenade grew terribly heavy. *Enfin,* our leafy tunnel brought me to my goal, and Savarin to his.

Here were some excellent truffles which the animal apparently considered the point of our dangerous journey. Without so much as a worshipful nod toward the L of J, K of P, Savarin fell to serious digging.

I lifted my binoculars to my eyes, training them on the moon-silvered clearing and compound.

It was a far cry from the day I'd baked my fabled soufflé; the dogs were at their posts beside *el jefe's* villa, and the lodge where Albion slept with the men was guarded by the most sadistic of my former jailers, who sat on the ground outside; through the window above him, I could see a brightly lit table, round which caroused a motley crew—young Miguel, old One Tooth, the lobotomy case, Albion, and Julia. I focused my glasses on Julia, because she seemed to be doing most of the joking, occasionally flinging her head back in that wicked laugh I knew so well. The others, from all appearances, considered her their spiritual leader, and were utterly captivated, as well as drunk.

I lowered my binoculars and considered. The sight of a little old lady of seventy—even at a distance—with a rose in her teeth is disconcerting. But Julia, as I've indicated, was a woman of rare and enduring vivacity; I have to admit, the old girl carried it off.

The question remained, could I get past the guard in my terrorist costume? Or would he remember my face?

How, one might ask, could he possibly forget?

Behind me, Savarin diligently rooted.

Above, the full tropical moon beamed its falling sickness.

I'd simply have to wait until Albion stepped outside to get a breath of cool air, then send him a secret signal.

I tried to think of a secret signal. Was there not some bird or animal unique to the islands of Maine, whose call would alert only Albion?

Attempting a foolproof disguise, I pulled the beak of Sissie's desert hat down as far as possible over my eyes short of blinding, drew the rear curtains forward to cover chin, mouth, and nose, and safety-pinned my bizarre veil in place. Then, submachine gun raised, I stepped into the moonlight.

The guard got to his feet, casually nodding his weapon toward mine, as if long accustomed to so greeting his strange multinational colleagues from the hills.

In guttural Prussian tones, I said I had a message for the woman and must see her alone. Though my Berlin Spanish doubtless left much to desire, he understood whom I meant by "the woman" and disappeared into the lodge.

After several tense moments, Julia appeared, sans rose, gliding toward me with hand outstretched in her most charming hostess fashion.

"Gregory," she said with surprise, "why are you dressed as Rommel in the desert?"

"Julia," I whispered, "I'm here to save you."

"Dear boy, from what?"

I led her away from the lodge so we wouldn't be heard. "I'm building a raft."

"How thrilling. Just like *Kon-Tiki*."

"Get Albion, and we'll run for it."

"But Gregory, what would I do on a raft? I'm much better off here. It's terribly kind of you to think of me—you always were such a sweet boy. Now I promise I won't tell it was you dressed up like Rommel, and you can toddle off on your raft." She patted my cheek. "I really am desperately moved that you wanted to run off with poor Julia. How romantic. You will be careful, won't you? You're such a dreadful sailor." She squeezed my hand and turned back to the lodge.

"Will you send out Albion?" I whispered.

"If you like, dear boy."

I waited in the shadows.

Presently, the Mainer lumbered out, suspiciously.

"Whippoorwill! Whippoorwill! *Psssst* . . . over here."

He walked toward me with his odd rolling gait and eyed me blearily. "Did you sign on with them rebels?" he inquired.

"Albion, I've come to save you."

I felt his bleary eyes focus on my safety pin. "From what?"

"From slavery. From crime and captivity. I'm offering you freedom."

The man seemed unmoved; in fact, he hiccuped.

"I need your help," I said. "I'm building a raft, and I need you to steer it."

"I can believe you do," he admitted without a great deal of interest.

"You won't come?"

"'Tain't that I don't 'preciate your thinkin' on me." His inebriation thickened his eloquence somewhat. "But as the feller says, it don't amount to a Hannah Cook. I wouldn't even get me bait back."

"No, that's very true. All you'll get is gold, diamonds, pearls, rubies, and emeralds."

The list had a sobering effect.

"Gold?" he inquired.

"Seven sacks of it."

His unyielding countenance stirred; across his beady eyes moved the glint of Yankee thrift.

"Goodly sized sacks?" he inquired.

"Big as your head."

He removed his duck-billed cap, lifted a grimy hand to his coconut, and rubbed it mathematically, gauging circumference. "I might ruminate on it."

"No time to ruminate. You've got to come now."

He scowled, and shifted from one foot to the other. "What are me whacks?"

"Fifty-fifty. Now hurry, the guard's going to come out."

"I suppose it don't make no damn's-odds," he muttered morosely, "blow high or blow low."

"But first, we've got to save Fielding."

"From what?"

I was getting sick and tired of constantly being asked that question.

"If you want him," muttered Albion, "shift your sights a fathom or two to the left."

I followed the captain's gaze to the villa and lifted the binoculars to my eyes.

On the porch sat three figures—the Destroyer, *el jefe*, and Fielding. The Destroyer and *el jefe* looked much as they had when last I saw them, but Fielding was a changed human being.

Of the three wraiths of smoke rising from the three cigars on the veranda, his wraith was the liveliest; of the three self-satisfied faces around the cigars, his was the most deeply satisfied. I saw a vitality in his bearing which I'd only glimpsed the ghost of previously— when listening to the retired man's reminiscences of corporate entities he'd ruined in his prime. Reminiscence was, for Fielding, now a game of the past. He'd jumped feet foremost into the fray, and found a new lease on life.

I reflected that romance, though it might take ten years off a woman, didn't compare to whatever could take twenty off a man.

I mused on power—power of universal magnitude; on a table between them sat a globe, and though they brandished cigars and not knives, the Destroyer, *el jefe*, and Fielding were clearly carving the world in three portions.

"Right," I said to Albion, "let's go."

Reluctantly, the skipper followed me into the burrow of leaves. "You didn't say we would sail on four feet. I ain't goin' nowise on me hands."

"Gold, Albion. Seven sacks."

The dour sailor grunted and got down on his knees, following my lead, as I followed Savarin's.

"What in Godfrey Jesus is that?"

"That is Anthelme Brillat-Savarin."

"French," snorted Albion. "Are we supposed to crawl like lobsters in back of a little pork chop?"

"That little pork chop found the gold."

I wondered how long it would take before Albion's guard realized he'd lost his prisoner, but we were making fair progress in spite of the captain's grumbling.

"I won't do it," muttered the old Mainer. "I won't give up a good berth to whale around all night in the pucker-brush."

"Gold," I said, "pieces of eight."

This appeared to keep him mobile, in spite of his continual complaining. Each time I heard him falling behind I'd call back to him, "Pieces of eight, pieces of eight," until I started to sound like Long John Silver's parrot.

"'Tain't natural," said the sailor, "men owlin' round after an animal."

"Doubloons, Albion. Louis d'or, pagodas, and sovereigns."

We were nearing the Pont de la Concorde. Savarin paused on the quai to make sure our native hunter was gone, and then we raced across the clearing.

"'Tain't no way to fetch the turf," insisted the captain. But I knew I wouldn't lose Albion now. He was unbeatable on water, but not much of a land navigator; he'd never find his way back alone through thorn hedge and pig roads.

As if he too were aware that his options had narrowed, he stopped grumbling quite so vociferously, but he was breathing loudly from the unusual effort of creeping and the duration of our nighttime hike through mountains.

"Slow down, Savarin," I said.

Naturally, Savarin didn't slow down. Though I liked to believe he understood and enjoyed my stories, I never received any indication that he comprehended commands.

"Try French," suggested Albion dryly.

In the distance, rockets exploded.

"We've had the pork," groaned the captain.

"You'll get used to it," I replied airily.

"You didn't tell me we was in for torpedoes."

Savarin uttered a squeal, and we hurried after his waddling form, down the low-lying hills to the cove and our cave in the orchids.

My Cartier watch read 4 a.m.

The first rays of dawn found us ensconced in the grotto, Albion's head and mine each resting on three sacks of treasure; the seventh lay midway between us.

Savarin munched a tuber.

"Have one," I said to the skipper.

"I'd liefer not," he grunted, eyeing the vegetable dubiously, but took a tentative nibble.

Then he took a second.

He bit into it greedily.

He glanced grudgingly at Savarin. "That's a handy beast."

"Finds gold too," I reminded him.

The captain accepted another tuber, surveying Savarin with less hostility. "Beats any pig I knowed Down East," he admitted.

"I don't believe he's actually a pig."

The old man adjusted his duck-billed cap. "No," he agreed, "he's more like somethin' from them history books."

Which is basically what I myself felt; that Savarin was some sort of throwback, to a time before man, perhaps, when animals were the brains of the earth. The fact that there were other such beasts on the island—as indeed there must've been, judging by the vast network of pigways— didn't alter my conviction of Savarin's uniqueness.

"Could be," mused Albion, "he's one of them pigadillos."

On this scientific summation, we went to sleep.

19

THE OLD SEA TURTLE GAZED OUT OVER THE WATER
as one who sees the court of Neptune, or in any case, the
tide and the wind.

We'd finished our breakfast, and I was showing him the
shallow cove from which I intended to launch our raft once
we'd built it. "Will we make it?" I asked.

"Not from here we won't."

So began our search, scouring the uninhabited side of the
island, Albion judging the various waters to determine our
best route to the ocean.

The man wasn't really comfortable on land, and perhaps
that explains his suspicions of one who dug in the earth so
enthusiastically; but he sensed Savarin's importance where
he himself was out of his element, as guide through the
steaming jungle.

"Puts me in mind," he said, after we'd spent much of the
day following the animal's confident passage through leafy
tunnels, "of a goat I use to know."

Though I could see nothing in Savarin the slightest bit
goatish, I felt the captain's comparison revealed a small
degree of growing trust.

The real Albion was hard to know, hidden deep within
the mysterious Down Easter, a breed more inscrutable than
any ten Chinamen. In him lurked the storms and lulls of
the sea; he was the ancient mariner, and I wondered what
albatross he killed to have landed his crew in this mess.

"Have you ever built a raft before?" I asked him.

"Daow," he answered tersely.

Now what sort of information was "daow"? I was beginning to suspect that if, somehow, I finally pierced Albion's core, I'd find a second Albion, tough as the first.

What was worse, in his presence I always felt I would make knot-tying errors at which the old turtle would scoff. The main thing, I decided, is to avoid tying knots; any time a knot should appear in the offing, I must find some urgency to call me away for the duration.

Nearby mortar fire interrupted my psychological analysis.

"Them rebels," remarked Albion, "appear to be a dite aggravated about somethin'."

"They're aggravated about me," I replied as explosives echoed in the next ravine. "They have a mistaken view of my character."

Or did they? After all, I had my captain and my pig, my gun and grenade; wasn't I therefore in command of my own small army?

A bullet whizzed through the bushes above us.

"I fear a fierce nor'wester," muttered Albion.

I feared Sissie and oil of coconut.

A second bullet denuded our bushes from the opposite direction.

Savarin stopped and circled, confused. They were gunning us down fore and aft; whichever way we went meant a cheekful of lead.

"I knowed that beast would bag the bowline," declared dour Albion.

The animal gazed at me piteously. *Why have you gotten me into this?* he seemed to ask. Then his beady little eyes grew hard. I could see the wheels of his intelligence turning, could see the profound exertions of an ancient creature struggling to understand racial memory, the lore of his ancestors, and their ancestors, and the earliest Savarins who'd dwelled on this primordial island aeons ago.

He sniffed the ground and the leaves, while the ever tightening military ring bombarded us from all angles.

His paws tore at the low underbrush.

Savarin disappeared.

"Follow him," I cried to the captain, and dove into the hole in the earth after my animal. "Man overboard," muttered the skipper, diving in our wake and grabbing onto my foot for guidance; the tunnel was totally black, and only the sound of Savarin's snuffles and the narrow walls of the channel itself directed us forward.

"We're suckin' the nether teat now," moaned Albion, his be-whiskered and denture-free diction further disfigured by a mouthful of earth.

I, of course, possessed the advantage of having undergone such an ordeal once before, and this tunnel, compared to my first, was luxuriously wide. How many Savarins must've dug it, working in teams, for years, maybe generations, to construct this porcine subway system?

"The Old Scholar's callin' me aft," groaned Albion.

"Just hang on to my foot."

Savarin was squeaking ecstatically, as though he'd found the lost city of the Incas, the fabled El Dorado of burrows. Far off, gunfire sounded impotently.

"I druther be shot than wizzle away underground."

"Pieces of eight, Albion, pieces of eight."

"Ayuh. If we don't coil our ropes first."

Since I was carrying gun and grenade, my progress wasn't fast, but Savarin seemed in no hurry either, now he'd discovered this wonderful place.

"'Tis the luck of Hiram Smith," said the skipper mournfully.

One wondered about the luckless Smith, but knew one's curiosity would never be slaked, because the old Mainer's reference points were deep and obscure as Savarin's tunnel.

Sightless, but with the faith of a mystic, I followed my remarkable animal. So finely constructed was this ancient burrow that breathing presented no difficulty; I suspect that the engineers who designed it must've perforated the ground above with invisible ventilation holes.

My admiration for Savarin, and the entire tribe of Savarins, already quite high, rose to near worship.

"Does she never end?" groaned the captain.

I felt sure it must end somewhere, but from all appearances so far, it just went on and on, twisting here, turning there, meandering.

Suppose we spent days in the place? Forever after I'd have to wear tinted glasses, and when asked about them would reply, "Too much time in the sewers during the war." (It's a line I've always wanted to use, but up until now could never claim a truly active part in the Resistance.)

"Man was meant to float on water," quoth Albion, "not crawl in the sod."

The view was a new one to me and gave pause for thought.

"Suppose she backwaters?" inquired the skipper.

The idea hadn't struck me before, that the tunnel of tunnels might turn around, doubling back on itself, and come out again in the same place. After all—and now I too grew fearful—there was really no way of telling what an extinct race of burrowers might've considered an elegant jest.

No sooner had this crisis of faith occurred, then Savarin stopped with a sharp squeak, as if he'd bumped into something hard.

I myself bumped into his tail. Albion bumped into mine.

The animal rose on his hindquarters and pawed overhead. I'd never known him to behave so bizarrely and feared he was reverting to wildness, but gradually his strenuous pawing produced . . . a glimmer of blessed light from above.

"Thanks be," muttered the captain.

Snuffling loudly, Savarin clawed at the brush above, until his entire incomparable snout was bathed in effulgence.

The extraordinary beast clambered upward, his forequarters disappearing through the exit, then with a slushing, heaving, churning motion, his hindquarters, and finally his formidable tail.

There were no sounds of gunfire.

No human voices.

Just the impatient Savarin, who peered back down into the tunnel as if to ask what we waited for.

I climbed out as well as I could, flinging my exhausted

person onto the grass; that dear Savarin placed his wet snout in my dirty hand as if wishing to say how glad he was to have saved me again.

We were on the edge of a pellucid pool, completely surrounded by forest except for a single narrow channel seaward. Possibly we were the first human beings who'd ever been there, since it was unreachable by land and invisible from the main body of water; the ducks and seagulls continued their bobbing as if they'd never been hunted, and the fish swam about unafraid, in great rainbow schools, beneath the green crystal surface.

"I'll be blowed," whistled Albion. "The pig provides."

I gazed after the old salt's pointing finger toward the base of the opposite cliff.

There, in the pool at the edge of the rocks, the oddest boat I'd ever seen was drifting aimlessly, with no one in it.

"She's parted her fasts," said the skipper.

"I beg your pardon."

"She's broke from her moorin' and washed up in this coodle."

I followed his bowlegged march around the edge of the cliff until we came close to the vessel, Savarin waddling behind, excitedly snooting. A parrot screamed from the thicket.

We leapt down from the grass to the beach and waded out to examine the native boat. The tropical sun burned the back of my neck, the water cooled my legs, Savarin squeaked from the beach, and I felt a precognitive sick roll in my stomach; how I'll miss that beast after I'm gone.

The vessel was a bit like a dugout canoe, with an enormous cleaverlike foot at one end; inside, it was lined with planks to form a double skin.

Not perhaps a showy boat; but miracle enough.

"She's a strange craft," admitted Albion, "but she'll round the Horn."

How quaint are these Maine expressions, I thought. Imagine saying "round the Horn" to indicate that a lightweight skiff is capable of navigating a few miles of calm Caribbean.

"I've always thought I might like to," mused the skipper. "Never had the 'tunity before."

"Like to what?" I inquired.

"Are ye deaf? Round the Horn."

"But Albion, I want to go home."

"I'm taken with the idear," replied he. "You must've heard tell of Joshua Slocum, first man to sail the world solo? He was me great-grand-uncle, thrice removed, or thereabouts."

"Couldn't we just sail to the next island but one?"

"The Horn is callin'. The roarin' forties and the Strait of Magellan."

"Not the roarin' forties, for God's sake. It's just a raft, Albion."

"Didn't you never hear tell of *Kon-Tiki?*"

"Last night, as a matter of fact."

"Well, that's us."

"That's news to me."

"I'm captain," said Albion succinctly.

20

WE SPENT SEVERAL DAYS IN THAT ENCHANTED lagoon, because, to be frank, neither of us was anxious to go back through the tunnel. If it hadn't been for the treasure, we wouldn't have returned inland at all, and the final tragedy might've been avoided.

But greed has always been man's ruination; it's the moral of this story, and of every other.

Albion spent his time fashioning paddles and oars, as well as a weird-looking mainsail from a burlap flour sack which drifted in on the second night's tide. He hoped to cruise the coast by boat and, ultimately, avoid the tunnel completely, retrieving our gold and water jugs and provisions without setting foot on land more than was minimally necessary.

Idle hands, they said, idle thoughts. Such was my position, exploring this beautiful and isolated landscape. Between the beach and the cliff, a ragged strip of blackened coral lay strewn with big pink conch shells and pale green cacti, like a garden of the moon. Within the virgin forest, towering mahogany, cedar, and perfumed eucalyptus rose from lacy doilies of blue forget-me-nots. Here was Eden, the untroubled peaceable kingdom; or so it seemed.

It was, as usual, Savarin who showed me different.

Though he liked to stay close beside me, his gourmet rooting often lured him several yards off into deeper woods. And at these times I was the follower, crawling warily through the bush, calling softly, "Savarin, oh, Anthelme, where are you?"

He'd answer with a squeal.

I'd creep to the sound of his voice.

Reunion would ensue, and I'd help with the rooting.

On this fateful occasion, I was about to give my soft call when the beast himself, eyes phosphorescent with fear, came barreling toward me from out of the brush.

"What is it?" I asked him.

He burrowed his face in my chest, his entire fat person shaking like *oeufs en carrousel*. I listened intently.

Only the song of a tree frog came from the thicket.

Savarin lifted his face, gazed at me, and slowly turned, to lead me back to that which had frightened him.

Why would he want to go back? you may ask.

Because, quite simply, he liked to share everything with me—that which pleased him, that which amused him, and that which scared him.

I knew it couldn't be a snake; Savarin wouldn't return to the embrace of a snake, nor would the little tree frog be singing so joyously.

Sounds of gunfire were far away; one could hardly hear them. No human was waiting for me in the bush, I felt sure.

I crept behind the animal's tail, alongside a fine freshwater ribbon, no more than a runoff from the mountain, hardly worth calling a brook. The tree frog sang and the rivulet murmured; there was nothing ominous in the scene, until the Thing itself was upon us, standing thirty feet tall, black and sleek, and covered with faces, its myriad sightless eyes gazing down on our trembling forms.

It took me several long moments to realize that what we'd come upon was a petroglyph, that giant slab of monumental sculpture carved by Indians untold epochs ago.

To come upon a lost work of art is indeed a religious experience; without thinking, I slowly pressed my palms together, while the ancient stone stared down at the first human being to kneel at its feet in the ages and ages which had passed since the last fierce Carib had worshipped here. Its hundred eyes seemed sad, with the sadness of bottomless patience; it had waited all these centuries to be worshipped again and now it must be satisfied with a broken decorator at the end of his tether and one ambiguous pig. Once we crept away, it would resume its sad slow vigil.

My own eyes grew moist. Needless to say, the Gregory Pluckrose of old would've made immediate plans for transporting the thing to the Museum of Natural History, with much fanfare and personal glory, articles in every important art journal of the world, a sinecure for life, and so on ad nauseum.

But to the Pluckrose I had become, such an idea, if it occurred at all, would've appeared impossibly vulgar. A bag of coins lifted from under unwitting pirates is one thing; an immemorial testament to the mystery of life is another.

To cut this painful scene short, let me say as briefly as possible, my discovery that a great civilization had flourished, believed, come to grief, and been forgotten by time and history, on this spot I'd considered merely an unspoiled setting for a picnic, produced the profoundest emotions in me.

I was devastated. (Perhaps Savarin was too, but I didn't wish to intrude on his feelings.)

I underwent all the usual embarrassing epiphanies—cosmic loneliness, insignificance, utter emptiness, and overwhelming compassion.

What did my petty survival matter?

There was only one thing that mattered, in this vast indifferent universe, and that was trying to help one's brothers.

(Forgive me for being so tasteless; nothing's more boring than goodness, but you must admit I haven't indulged overmuch in this virtue.)

My mind was in a passionate state.

I must, I saw, save my friends—Julia, Fielding, and Sissie.

Well, maybe not Sissie.

Julia then, and Fielding.

Definitely Julia.

What sort of life was it for that dear, sweet, silly woman,

stranded on a criminal island with filthy smugglers, pirates, and rebels? She belonged in a tea shop in L-port.

The situation had to be remedied.

The Lord of the Jungle must take action.

The reasonable reader may here protest that Julia didn't wish to be saved. But when do religious fanatics ever consider other people's wishes? Revelation is always stronger than reason. And mine was thirty feet high, carved in primordial stone, with a hundred melancholy eyes.

Fanaticism and greed. I knew, even in my overwrought state, that nothing but gold would lure Albion inland. I'd have to keep my plans for kidnapping Julia a secret.

Right, Savarin?

21

ALBION MOVED OUR BOAT TO A LAGOON LESS remote and protected than the place with the petroglyph, a tactical error in my opinion, but the claustrophobic old seaman refused to "keep burrowin' through underground tunnels like a Godfrey Mighty clam."

He also had his own firm theory on transporting provisions. "Better to pack-and-back than lug the stuff."

The distinction was this:

To lug meant to make separate trips for our sacks of treasure, water bottles, and so forth; to pack-and-back meant to lug each item just a short way, then return for the next, bring it up to the first, carry the first a little further, go back to where we'd left the second, and on in this manner. In the end, I suppose it came to half as many long trips, but it certainly seemed to entail a hundred frustrating short ones.

All of this labor had to be accomplished under cover of darkness because of gunfire and bombardment, and several encounters would've proved fatal to us had not Savarin—as even Albion admitted—held a trick or two up his sleeve, in the way of ever more recondite pig roads.

We loaded our boat at dawn, that silent cool moment in the tropics when moon and sun are poised on either horizon.

Tubers and mangoes, passion fruits and bananas, cashews, coconuts, breadfruits, and guavas made up our store. Along with treasure and water, this didn't leave much room for extra passengers, but I had the messianic urge to save Julia, and nothing could stop it.

"We'll shore off with the evenin' tide," said the captain, covering the vessel at anchor with hanging foliage, a pretty disguise, which gave me an idea for my own.

Obviously, I couldn't return to the compound in my guerrilla costume, because I'd used it once. Rommel of the desert would not pass unchallenged a second time.

I must go disguised as vegetation.

With consummate care, I attired myself in green banana fronds, pink oleander, scarlet flamboyant, purple moonflower, and aromatic eucalyptus leaves. Floral arrangements are my forte, and I was performing an outstanding job, considering lack of mirror and other amenities.

"Where in tunket are you preachin'?" inquired the skipper.

"I must save Julia," I coolly informed him.

"'Tain't likely," he said thoughtfully. "Not unless you twist her tail."

"Then I shall twist her tail."

"Or catch a crab."

"I shall take her by force if necessary." (Dear God, the things one says when in the grip.)

Albion perused my floral ensemble and remarked he personally wouldn't wear same to a dogfight.

I gazed meaningfully at his own oversized overalls and duckbilled cap.

"What should I do," he asked, "if you don't come back?"

"When is the evening tide?"

"Five bells."

"At five bells, you may sail. With or without me." (I felt this heroic statement to be utterly worthy of all the Grade B films of my childhood, and indeed probably stole it directly.)

In my ravishing attire I set forth on my quest at sunset; Albion yawned and remarked, "I suppose I'll hit the felt."

Savarin the Indomitable accompanied me on my journey, considerably slowing his waddle to the pace of a man in a vegetable suit.

We crept through the brush I'd grown to detest; what

luxury it would be to walk erect, as man was made, on God-given sidewalk.

Why, then, am I risking my life? I wondered.

Why bother?

Fielding will be impossible to galvanize, and as for Julia . . .

Julia is a civilized woman. I will remind her of our shopping dates in L-port, and she will be glad to quit the depravity of this place. I must save Julia. It's the only decent thing to do. The poor woman cannot be left on a foreign shore to the mercy of ruthless men.

I felt as if I were rescuing my own mother, almost.

We crossed the Pont de la Concorde, made for the Champs Elysées, and soundlessly approached *el jefe's* compound.

At the junction of jungle and clearing, where those excellent tubers grew, Savarin refrained from rooting, but remained resolutely at my side, as if sensing the danger of the moment and how short was our time left together.

I lifted my binoculars from the leafy folds of my person and trained them on the lodge, above the drowsy guard outside, in through the brightly lit window to the chamber where last I'd seen Julia, rose between teeth.

The tableau that met me was a sad one.

Miguel, old One Tooth, and the lobotomy case sat around the cluttered plank table, gazing gloomily at each other, plunged in deepest mourning. The man with the scar, particularly, seemed to feel life was not worth living; each time he lowered his bottle from his dribbling lips, he shook his dim-witted head in despair. The room itself was a bachelor shambles; there were certainly no roses in the vase on the table. As I watched, the man with the scar lifted the empty vase, stared at it peculiarly, and smashed it furiously to the ground.

I grabbed Savarin, who squeaked in surprise.

Was she dead then? My darling Julia.

Whom else could they be mourning?

I must find out.

But how?

I couldn't knock on the lodge door and ask. Perhaps if I

could get to the villa, if I could see Fielding . . . he would tell me.

Slowly, I crept along the edge of the jungle toward the inner compound; the guard dogs stopped their prowling to sniff suspiciously at the air. And here the heroic Savarin performed his greatest act of valor; that loyal creature, sensing my need to go forward, used himself as a decoy to sidetrack the dogs.

Rather like Marie Antoinette approaching the guillotine, Savarin marched, head held high, to the hounds.

In an instant they were upon him, and he was leading them a merry chase through the thorn hedge. (Naturally, they didn't stand a chance, being domesticated animals, against the primeval Savarin, and Savarin knew it, had probably been teasing these dogs for generations.)

Shaken but determined, I walked across the manicured grounds, forming tasteful flower arrangements with each new shrub and flower bed in my path.

I had to proceed with excruciating slowness over the bare tracts of lawn, but once I reached a grouping of blossoms or specimen tree, so perfect was my decorator's sense (this is no time for false modesty) that none of the guards noticed the addition of one more bush. So effective were my designs that the single dog who hadn't chased Savarin lifted his leg against mine, and watered my foliage.

I entered the inner circle of the court and drew near the villa, the arrangements of flower bed and bush becoming ever more intense and interesting.

I froze in the downward-cascading arms of a shower-of-gold tree, composing myself among its yellow buds and petals so artistically that it's really a shame no one was there with a camera.

I disentangled my binoculars from herbiage, and focused on the dining room window.

Within, around Waterford crystal and demitasse, sat:

El jefe—small and immaculate in tailored cocoa linen, his wizened coffee-brown face alive with that terrible intelligence, his oversized hands clenching and opening convulsively on the Belgian lace cloth, his arms steeped in hallucinatory blood, his eyes blinking like the heartbeats of his myriad victims.

The Destroyer—wearing a black suit and tie, against which the white of his shirt and the white of his teeth glittered mercilessly. His darkly hooded eyes had the look of a boa constrictor digesting an antelope twelve times its size, a meal of the most exquisite sweetness.

Fielding—looking much as he had when first I'd met him—a ruddy-faced bulldog of a gentleman in semiretirement, still consulted by governments and large corporations and on the verge of saying something fascinating and profound, which never quite comes out.

And Julia—wearing a saintly, almost frail demeanor, as if she'd been through a very great ordeal, but would, with costly pampering, gallantly pull through. She also wore several fortunes in jewels at her surgically lifted bosom and ears, and her marvelous talonlike fingers were once more bedecked with heirloom brilliants.

I can't say that she did most of the talking, but she was clearly the centerpiece—the delightful, birdbrained, vivacious, and utterly charming lady of the old school—a school on the brink of extinction, a school to be cared for and cherished, a school of breeding and fineness so fragile and dazzling that the two swarthy lords of the Third World were really quite touched; almost honored.

Obviously nothing she said was of importance; the three kings of commerce and industry listened in the most cavalier and superior way. But oddly, each time she finished, one or another of the men seemed to be struck by a powerful and original brainstorm, which set the three giants to intense conversation on lofty subjects—I couldn't hear, but the visual impression was unmistakable—while dear silly Julia played with her priceless rings and smiled appreciation of men's minds.

My retinal rods protruded practically to the point of popping out and shattering the lenses of my binoculars.

I couldn't believe what I was seeing.

What, you may ask, was I seeing?

I shall tell you:

I was seeing that men are fools.

Certainly Fielding was a fool. He'd been ruled by his wife all his life. All his crushing of competitors' bones was merely his working interpretation of Julia's suggestions; perhaps she never came out and said, "Dear, would you please break so-and-so's back? Would you suck poor Binkie's blood and drain him dry for me?" But she showed Fielding how to conquer; she led him elegantly along the difficult and subtle pathways of trusts, monopolies, and international conglomerates.

Certainly *el jefe* was a fool. In his own villa, on his own island, where he'd done quite well for himself, he was being commanded by a captive.

The Destroyer was the worst fool of all: a sheik with his own private navy, torpedoed by a Chestnut Hill dowager.

And I too, I was a fool.

Had I really wanted to leave my easy and richly remunerative job with Fuffie Blunt?

Had I ever wished to take a cruise, I the least boaty of men?

How had I let myself become omelette and *potage* chef, I who never lifted a finger for a client before, unless it was to raise a delicate corner of Rose Cumming chintz?

And yet, I'd risked my life twice for a woman of seventy.

Not only that, but I wasn't finished risking.

Because after all was said and done, I still didn't know, for sure, whether the dear woman really was evil. Might she not be good— underneath it all?

And didn't I need to save her now more than ever? Now it was not merely her aged body I was saving, but her soul.

Having inspired her three slave-kings to think along the route she desired, having instilled her murderous ideas in their masculine minibrains, Julia now rose from her seat, with fluttering respect, and offered to leave them alone to their Olympian discussions, and the more gory details, while she, frail saint, stepped out for some air.

How protective they were.

They must wrap her in shawls.

They must kiss her glittering hands.

They must puff themselves with consideration until they looked like a trio of macho balloons.

Julia glided out to the veranda, and sat herself down on a rattan banquette with a delightfully wicked sigh.

How could one not adore her?

I blended myself with the trellis and shimmied up to the porch; then, to her wondering eyes, a beautiful bud-bedecked bush separated itself from the tropical foliage.

"Gregory," she said with surprise, "why are you disguised as vegetation?"

"Julia, I've come to save you."

"Dear boy, again?"

"Albion and I have a boat. We're sailing at five bells, and you must sail with us."

"You know, I'm terribly annoyed with you, Gregory. If you'd only been patient, I could"ve convinced them to give you a job in the kitchen, and by now we'd be redecorating the villa together. But it's going to be so much more difficult. Why did you have to make yourself so unpopular? Using up all of *el jefe's* Bijan and drinking his 1846 Château Lafite. What a mess you left, I never would've believed it. My dear, I can't understand what in the world you ever wanted with Sissie's shirt. She's not even your size. You've made your position on this island dreadfully problematical. Why, oh why couldn't you have trusted to Julia?"

"Quick, we must flee."

"But dear boy," she murmured with missionary zeal in her eyes, "I need you here," She gazed into my face with the most lively interest, her cornflower orbs bright with plans. I could see, she wanted to redo not just the villa—but me.

My illusions crumbled. That rare and lovely polish which Julia's skin seemed always to wear, I now perceived, was the shine of her secret steel.

I knew the truth. The game had come to its final square, and my only possible move was flight and survival.

(What outrage, exactly, had she in mind? I cannot say, but any form of lackeyhood was less than attractive to He who ran free as Lord of the Jungle. No, I must follow my own ideas now, the principal one being to escape with my life.)

"I'll tell you what," she said. "We'll explain the entire situation to *el jefe*. You'll apologize for stealing his suit, his watch, and his favorite Panama hat, and everyone will let bygones be bygones." As she spoke, I glanced in through the window at the dining room table and the gentleman who was supposed to let bygones be bygones; *el jefe's* glowering eyes met mine, and in that flickering instant, I saw all the grim events of the old man's life, his full brutal power, all that had stained his wizened arms to the elbows. Soursop ice cream spilled down my spine as I met the eyes of the ultimate outlaw, who would hold the whole earth in bondage.

El jefe snapped his oversized fingers; guards burst through the doorway with drawn submachine guns.

In a quick series of floral arrangements, I leapt from the veranda and departed, to the accompanying cries of "Do try to shoot low" from dear Julia.

Bullets whizzed over my head as I merged tastefully into the shower-of-gold tree, then into a royal palm festooned with orchids, a fragrant frangipani, and so on across the lawn.

Grenades exploded in back of my fronds, as I dove into the pig path, behind the faithful Savarin, who'd manifested at the first shout of "Do try to shoot low" and the rather conflicting call from *el jefe, "Amatto! Amatto!"*

We scurried as never before, with dogs and guns on our trail, not across the Pont de la Concorde, but straight through the jungle in a totally new (to me) thorn hedge burrow.

Did Savarin know where we were going?

Did he know that if I wasn't at the boat by five bells, Albion would leave alone, and I'd be rendered to coconut-scented massage oil, bottled, and sold in a sex shop in Miami?

I glanced at my Cartier watch.

My heart practically failed.

Five bells had come, and passed. So intrigued had I been, watching the scene in the dining room, that I'd lost track of the bells altogether.

It was over.

. . . Unless Albion had waited, which, given Albion's hard shell and the hard kernel of Albion I suspected underneath the hard shell, he hadn't.

Furious with myself for having wasted time with Julia, for having thrown over my last chance at escape, I followed Savarin through pickers and thorns, my attractive floral arrangement debased and torn beyond recognition.

The gunfire sounded now further to our left, as if our pursuers had taken the wrong trail. But what did it avail to one who was doomed?

Spirit crushed, illusions shattered, vegetable suit a disgrace, I crawled behind my animal while the forest resounded with grenades. I sensed that Sissie was now on the job; no one else could make such loud and vulgar explosions.

The new route wandered past a cool waterfall, and I was tempted to lie down and die.

But Savarin trotted forward, and I followed.

Giant ferns slapped my face. The game was played. The queen had checkmated me. And I didn't even know chess; nor bridge; nor backgammon; nor tennis; nor tiddly winks; nor any of the other aggressive pastimes a normal childhood teaches. While other kids shot craps, I made floral arrangements. And here was the bitter fruit.

Half dead with despair, creeping on my belly like a snake, I blindly pawed my way through the jungle until we came to a clearing. My life was passing before me. (Oh no, I sighed, not again.)

A seagull circled the moonlight above me. Have we come to the sea then? I wondered. I can drown myself. The sooner the better. I crawled along the grass to the beach, with the same old visions of Syrie Maugham sofas, marble-topped bronze-doré commodes, and bosky eighteenth-century Chinese wallpaper flashing through my wearied brain.

"You're three bells late," remarked Albion.

"Albion," I gasped, "is it you?"

"So far as I can determine."

"You waited," I gasped with emotion.

"I always was number'n a hake. Now will you hark your whimperin' and get in the dinghy."

I wondered whether Albion's life was flashing by him; probably not. Dour and practical as ever, the old Mainer was setting his sail, and our race to freedom was merely another day's work in a long life of days, or nights; it's the tide that rules a sailor's life.

"Good-bye, Savarin," I cried, "good-bye, old friend."

I stepped into the boat and heard the very loud retort of a motor beside me.

"Albion, you found a motor!"

"You might put it that way."

"You stole it."

"Nothin' else to do while you was off gaffin' the old lady."

"Oh, Albion," I said, as the motor began to putt-putt us to freedom, "she is a wicked woman."

"They're a weakly sex," he remarked tolerantly, which went to show that though the old salt knew everything about the ocean, his land experience had never quite jelled.

We puttered across that lovely cove in the moonlight as if Albion had navigated these shores all his life. Back on the beach stood Savarin, his beady eyes straining after our craft, his chubby figure growing smaller and smaller. I saw him turn around, circling his tail in confusion, then waddle to the edge of the sea, and point his rubbery snout at the lonesome moon.

I saw his little mouth open in a mute squeak of sorrow, and then he tumbled face forward on the sand, his brave heart broken.

"Stop," I cried to the captain. "We're going back."

"We daren't."

"We can't leave Savarin."

"Nor we can't have a pig for a dory-mate. 'Tis bad luck to even use the word on a ship."

"But Savarin's not a pig."

"Close enough to."

The gunfire from the jungle grew louder, though we were almost clear of the inlet and I could barely distinguish the stricken figure bunched on the sand.

"Albion, it was Savarin who found the gold."

Albion steadied his hand on the throttle; the boat stopped moving. I could see the old Mainer's sense of fairness warring against superstition. "That don't mean a three-way split?"

"Fifty-fifty."

There was a long ruminative pause, and then the old skipper turned the craft in the water, and we began to putt-putt back toward the dark shore and the ever intensifying sound of machine guns. "All this niddy-noddin'," muttered Albion, "almost enough to aggravate a feller."

As the roar of our motor grew closer, the fallen figure of Savarin started to rise; he stumbled forward into the sea, and his snout, raised aloft like a snorkel, slowly drifted toward us.

"B'God, he floats," said the skipper, with the closest thing to respect I'd ever heard in his voice; or ever would again.

We met the aquatic creature and lifted him up into the boat by his forepaws just as Sissie and her squad of underprivileged street fighters swarmed out of the jungle and ran for the beach.

"Let's get humpin'," ordered the captain, opening the motor as far as it would go. A shower of gunfire pursued us, and then I heard a mercenary cry: "To the harbor!"

Needless to say, our little canoe filled with heavy provisions wouldn't be much of a match for the power craft and warship in *el jefe's* harbor.

"Faster," I begged the motor.

"She's clippin' about as fast as she can. Just the same as a toad in a tar bucket."

Savarin lay on his back in the bottom of our vessel, heaving short rasping sighs; I suspect that his abilities as a swimmer hadn't been tested in a few million years. I slipped my hand in his paw, feeling the little claws weakly close round my fingers; he gazed up at me dully.

"Alst we need," muttered Albion, "is for the engine to cag out."

"Is it cagging?"

"I don't like her voice," he admitted, as we rounded the crooked peninsula that formed one jaw of the crocodile-shaped harbor.

The stolen yachts lay still in the moonlight; a more beautiful group of sloops, yawls, and ketches you never saw. The rebels were marining the launches, but the launches didn't appear to be moving.

"Why aren't they after us?" I asked.

"Hard to set chase when your motor's got sand in her."

"But why would the motors have sand in them?"

"Dunno," he replied thoughtfully. "Some old trigger must of sanded them."

Howls of anger came from the launches. Sissie and Colonel Goose-step and several of the more gung-ho killers set after us in a rowboat.

At that instant our engine cagged out.

"What now?" I cried.

"I'll row. You shoot."

"I don't know how to shoot."

"Then why in tunket do you tow that dumbie around with you?"

Though Albion was a better oarsman than any of the mercenaries, they were stronger in number, and the distance between us was narrowing, the bullets coming dangerously close.

I aimed my submachine gun at the oncoming vessel, but the gun did not fire.

"Hurl your grenade," hollered the captain.

I yanked the grenade from the folds of my palm fronds, pulled the pin, and gazed at it.

"She's gonna blow," shouted Albion. "You've pulled the pin, you've gotta throw her!"

Little did he know he was talking to a person who'd cut

and sewn costumes while other children were out tossing
handballs; while others kicked the pigskin, I was collecting
theatrical *memorabilia;* while others pitched and batted,
I was home rearranging the furniture for mother's mah-
jongg party. (Every week it was different; her friends were
jade with envy; but it did not further my gifts for flinging
grenades.)

"She's sputterin'," yelled the captain as the thing in my
hand started to sizzle.

I wound up my arm, as I'd seen in *The Dizzy Dean Story,*
and aimed for the plate. The grenade bobbled on the air,
and sank in the sea, midway between us and the rebels. I
had failed.

Two seconds later, we felt a muffled explosion and the
enemy rowboat started to sink.

"You whaled her," cried Albion. "You struck her from
underneath. By the old Lord Harry, she's goin' down like a
drogher."

I wish you could've seen the expression on Sissie's
countenance when she realized she'd been done in by a
Pluckrose curve ball. (Oh well, it was good training for her.)

The gunboat went down, as Albion remarked, "slicker'n
a smelt," and the militia paddled around in the churning
water like so many sputtering faucets.

"Green to green," declared the captain with satisfaction.
"Now put your arse behind you, and paddle."

So he rowed, I paddled, and a fair wind caught our flour
sack mainsail. Gradually, Savarin recovered, and took his
seat in the stern, shiny snout pointed in the direction of his
vanishing homeland.

We Pluckroses are believers in fate. Its power has
been displayed time and again, but never so nobly and
harmoniously as in the sight of Savarin. He was the gift of
the islands, a pig of perfect proportion and a master of self-
preservation. Without him I would have been lobster stew,
and you may lay to that.

"He might come in handy," Albion admitted. "If the

rations get short, we can eat him. I think I'd fancy them cheeks."

This was too much for my already strained nerves. Something inside me snapped. I reached down to my Victorian lap desk, opened the secret compartment, and drew forth the silver letter opener from L-port.

Holding this instrument beneath Albion's surprised, grizzled chin, I whispered, "Touch that animal, and you're shark bait."

So, in that hour of darkness, I removed myself from the human race, by threatening my captain with mutiny and murder; practically patricide, if you consider our age difference.

"No need to get exercised," said the mariner. "I was just makin' pleasant conversation."

And, in truth, he didn't seem to hold it against me. Perhaps, during his time with the pirates, he'd seen many such differences of opinion argued with blade, broken bottle, and fist, or, perhaps, he was simply a person of large tolerance, an independent Yankee, in whose long experience, everyone was half cracked anyway.

* * *

Our voyage took a good time, since Albion was determined to emulate his great-grand-uncle, thrice removed, or thereabouts, and circumnavigate at least part of the world.

Many strange lands and red sunsets saw our bizarre little craft with its crew of two weather-beaten, rough-bearded men and an animal who always sat in the stern, its long snout pointing at that which was no longer visible, a place of distant dreams, of cool dappled streams, of bright waterfalls, and brilliant flowers, and dark verdant thorn hedge, and intricate, primordial burrows.

We anchored at many ports, keeping to the primitive, untraveled places, and were welcomed at the glowing campfires of generous natives.

On the whole, the three of us got on well in our tiny ship, Albion and I both compulsively neat, and Savarin, of course, unparalleled company. By sun and star we sailed, Albion's peaked cap ever fixing our bearing like some kind of compass without which we'd flounder; I grew strangely protective of this cap. Sharks circled the turquoise water, but Albion's tub was a match for them, and for all.

We rounded Cape Horn, and steered our course mainly nor'west, until one evening, in autumn, the skipper stroked his long gray beard, and mumbled, "I suppose." Then our odd little craft joined the bustling traffic moving under the Golden Gate Bridge, and San Francisco welcomed the three lost sailors. It was a cool evening, with the city's magnificent skyline framed in hibiscus-red smaze and low-flying gulls; so insignificant was our boat that no coast guard could have suspected we'd been out for more than an hour in such an unseaworthy vessel; this had been our disguise all along; only Albion's genius was capable of steering a wedge-footed canoe eight-thousand nautical miles. We dipped our flour-sack sail to the U.S.A.

And the great adventure was over.

EPILOGUE

Needless to say, when one considers the long arm of such as Fielding F. Hale, *el jefe,* and the Destroyer, my life as Gregory Pluckrose wasn't worth a Godiva chocolate. So I became Guillermo Jesus Manuel Cordero, ex-customs agent, who fled a repressive regime with the family fortune. (It isn't so very far off the truth.)

In order not to risk recognition in familiar surroundings, I settled on the West Coast. I quite fell in love with San Francisco, from our first breathtaking sight of her scarlet skyline and the first bath I took in our suite at the Mark Hopkins.

I bought a small Victorian-with-a-view in Pacific Heights, which I had the most divine time imaginable restoring; I'd never really had the wherewithal before to decorate a place of my own the way I wanted.

Albion, that dour seaman, drifted back to Maine, where he goes among his own relatives by the name of Guillermo Jesus Manuel Cordero, Senior; they must think it rather peculiar, but I suppose Albion's many relatives accept each other's eccentricities as philosophically as they do icy winds and cold seas; he's quite the figure among them, with his prize-winning bark, a beautiful square-rigged thing which he bought from someone who claimed to have found it adrift in the Caribbean; one wonders.

As for the others, whenever I read in the *Chronicle* of a small country being swallowed, or hear of a government toppling, I think of Sissie and her ridiculous army, and I imagine that dining room table, around which sat *el jefe,* the Destroyer, and my former employer, being led on a silken thread by the most delightful of spinners.

I promised myself I wouldn't bore you with a detailed description of my charming *pied-à-terre* in Pacific Heights, but I feel it's not unapropos to admit I succumbed to a bit of nostalgia in designing one tiny room.

I call it my cell.

It's a place of extreme intimacy, furnished with only a pillow-laden opium bed, a round copper stand, and a small Chagall on the wall.

When you tip the Chagall, you find a window, looking out upon the largest and deepest private garden in San Francisco, within whose thorn hedge borders dozes a fat little creature of indeterminate species but striking intelligence, a being of lofty nature and elegant tastes, a being who stretches and yawns, and lifts its rubbery snout to gaze at you standing framed in the window.

"Coming, Savarin."

About the Author

Elizabeth Gundy is the author of such highly praised novels as *Bliss*, *The Disappearance of Gregory Pluckrose*, and *Love, Infidelity and Drinking to Forget*. She also coauthored the bestselling children's series Walter the Farting Dog. She is married to the writer William Kotzwinkle.

OPEN ROAD
INTEGRATED MEDIA

Open Road Integrated Media is a digital publisher and multimedia content company. Open Road creates connections between authors and their audiences by marketing its ebooks through a new proprietary online platform, which uses premium video content and social media.

www.ingramcontent.com/pod-product-compliance
Lightning Source LLC
Chambersburg PA
CBHW020325260626
47156CB00004B/1385